I0532722

Emergence

HUGH A. FLOWERS

Copyright © 20156 Hugh A. Flowers
All rights reserved.

~~~~

No part of this book may be reproduced or transmitted or transferred in any form or by any means, graphic, electronic, mechanical, including photocopying, recording, taping or by any information storage retrieval system or device, without the permission in writing by the author
Any resemblance to actual people and events is purely coincidental.
This is a work of fiction.

Paperback-Press
an imprint of A & S Publishing
A & S Holmes, Inc.

ISBN-13: 978-0692702857
ISBN-10: 0692702857

TABLE OF CONTENTS

ACKNOWLEDGMENTS

I'd like to give a special thank you to Nathalie Kelley for once again painting the perfect cover art for this book. You did a wonderful job.

My thanks also goes out to Tina Vyborny for her help. Your time is appreciated.

Sharon Kizziah-Holmes, thank you for everything. You and Paperback-Press made publishing this book possible. You are a professional in every way.

.

CHAPTER ONE

The two Blues stood before the High Priestess of the Healing Guild at its world headquarters in Kansas City. The High Priestess was always given the name Angel Pearson, to honor the Guild's founder. She was a beautiful young woman dressed in a white flowing robe who was staring uncertainly at the two, then making her decision, she said, "Aaron, Alice, you are both from different locations, have you ever met before?"

They both answered they hadn't.

"You have been tested as having the strongest ESP gifts among all the Reds or Blues. I want you to start an undercover organization to ferret out anyone who would conspire against the Guild. I've received information about several individuals and organizations that have threatened to abduct and use our members for personal gain. This must not happen! Use this information and if true, check with me before taking any action. I have made arrangements for you to work and reside outside this building. I want you to go undercover and blend with the general public, don't dress as a Blue except when reporting here at my request. Normal reports are to be made mentally to my assistant, Director Natalie Bertram, who will provide you with the details of your mission."

The two Blues left the High Priestess and returned to the reception desk where Aaron asked for Director Natalie Bertram.

Arriving at their destination they looked at each other a moment before squaring their shoulders and entered the room and asked to see the Director. They were immediately shown inside where they stood waiting on her to finish a com call. The woman behind the desk appeared to be in her late twenties and was dressed as a Blue. She looked up and scrutinized them with penetrating gray eyes. "Ah, you must be Aaron and Alice. Apparently the Priestess has agreed with my recommendation for the department and your selection."

Director Bertram leaned back in her chair and was satisfied with her selection. Aaron was a head taller than Alice and although today was the first time they had met they seemed comfortable with each other, neither deferring to the other. Their clothing was the standard uniform of their station, a blue tunic and matching pants.

"Please call me Natalie when face to face or Control when speaking to me mentally. I have arranged civilian clothing for you to wear when you leave here. You will live and work out of your quarters and it is fully furnished except for personal items and clothing that you will acquire before starting your assignment. Also, you each will be provided an unlimited chit, come here so I can load it into your implant."

After this procedure was completed, Natalie told them to take a seat. "You both have alpha personalities, so you will have to work out how you divide tasks."

She tossed a comp device to Alice. "Insert that into your home vid unit and make yourself aware of its contents. When you have something to report, think CONTROL and I will respond. Do either of you have romantic attachments from your previous locations?"

Both Blues negatively shook their heads. Aaron asked, "How much expense leeway do we have in following leads that may require global travel?"

"If I feel it's appropriate, then you won't get a slap on the wrist. One of your stops today will be at this address." She placed a card on the desk.

"You need to be fitted with the latest in body armor that fits over your body from ankles to your neck. It's supposed to be like a second skin and protects you from all known hand projectile and laser weapons. Use your chit to pay for it, but let me know if you are charged more than the agreed price of 200,000 credits for the pair. If it fails to meet your requirements, let me know. Your apartment and code access information is on this card."

Alice said, "Funny! If someone shoots me and it penetrates the armor, do I ask for a refund? What if I need to pee? How do I get out of it?"

"Ask the vendor. They will answer your questions. If you have no other questions go through that connecting door and change into your street clothes. Leave your uniform behind. It will be cleaned and kept here for you when you return to see the Priestess."

Once inside the change room they viewed each other uncertainly until Alice shrugged her shoulders and started to disrobe to her underclothes. She folded her Blue uniform and placed it on a shelve, and then looked at the clothing left for her. It was a brief halter and a pair of shorts. Alice started to put them on, but when she turned to see Aaron's outfit she placed a hand over her mouth, smothering a laugh.

Aaron responded, "Yeah, these clothes are a joke. You can't even wear your bra with that halter and this shirt only comes down to just below my chest, and my shorts are almost as brief as yours. It's good that you don't need the support of a bra, but my outfit looks ridiculous on me."

"I don't know, with those abs of yours, it looks pretty good to me. Let's go show her what this looks like."

They walked back into Natalie's office and posed for her. She looked at them for a moment, before smiling at their discomfort. "That's the fashion for casual wear and you certainly don't look like a Blue anymore. Why don't you get fitted for your armor before buying yourselves some business wear clothing. You both need to change your shoes to those I got for you."

"Crap! I can't walk in those things, they won't stay on," Aaron said in disgust.

Alice said, "Come on, I think I can get them to work for you. We need to get out of here and get some real clothes."

When they left Guild Headquarters they both cringed as they stepped outside. Neither of them had much experience outside the closed society of the Guild where they had lived most of their lives. Aaron used his wrist comp to hail a robo cab, and after a short wait for its arrival, gave it the address of the armor vender. Kansas City, located on the banks of the Missouri River, reflected a population of over 18 million at the last census of 2310 and is the largest city in the Midwest, closely followed by Chicago.

Ground transportation was limited to public transports and robo cabs. Exceptions were police and emergency services, light and heavy transports, and occasional government vehicles. Twenty minutes later they were stopped at the vendor's location.

The storefront was advertised as *Amorer for the Masses*. The décor was displays of various body protections, which they checked out as they walked to the rear of the store. A black female clerk dressed in camo was hard to see and looked sinister in the dimly lit counter area. Aaron told her who they were and that they were there for a fitting.

The clerk checked her comp and used the intercom to summon help. Shortly, a man and woman arrived to escort them to their separate fitting rooms. Alice was asked to strip to her skin so that accurate measurements could be made, whereupon the female clerk used a hand scanner for the measurements. She was given a robe while waiting for the product to arrive.

Thirty minutes later Alice was given what the clerk called Silks, probably because that was what the material felt like. Alice sat and pulled the material over her feet and then her arms. The fitter told her to pull the material together in front and touch a tab at the neck, which caused the material to bond together seamlessly.

Alice looked at herself in the full-length mirror and the material seemed to disappear. She adjusted her breasts to her satisfaction." Wow! This stuff is amazing. It even supports my boobs. What do I need to do when I use the toilet?"

The fitter showed her a tab at her hip, which when touched allowed the material to be parted so that she could use the toilet. Alice was told that the material would leach her sweat and she should wear cotton underclothing over the silks to absorb these fluids. Air exposure would work as well.

Alice donned the minimal clothing she had arrived in and couldn't see any evidence of the Silks on her body. It was like a second skin that was invisible to the eye. Aaron and Alice returned to the counter and paid for their purchase before leaving to shop for clothing.

Neither of them were familiar with Kansas City stores, so they directed their robo cab to take them to the nearest high-end clothing store. Fifteen minutes later they were at a high-rise department store. Inside they found that the women and men's clothing departments were on different floors.

Aaron asked, "Do you want my input when you shop? I can certainly use yours for mine. Blues is all I've ever worn."

Alice smiled at him. "Let's do mine first because I've got a feeling that's going to be more difficult."

Six hours later they were in a robo cab with their purchases heading toward their apartment. The complex of buildings where they were dropped off was intimidating at first, but they soon found their apartment. It was located on the fifteenth floor of a thirty-story building. Their code got them into the lobby and thumbprint into their apartment.

The apartment had two bedrooms with baths, a common living area, and a small kitchen. Alice quickly lay claim to a bedroom and dropped her purchases on the bed. After checking the bath she called out, "Aaron, we need toiletries. Let's find somewhere to eat and get what we need on the way back."

He replied, "I found a sheet on the counter listing several restaurants and a pharmacy located within this complex. What do you want to eat?"

Alice came and looked at the listing. "I heard that Kansas City is noted for their bar-b-que and there's one here. Do you want to try it?"

"Okay, but I'm not wearing these shorts another minute."

Alice looked at his firm rear as he entered his bedroom before sighing in disappointment when the door closed. Thirty minutes later she met Aaron in the common room and they left for a late dinner. They both enjoyed their meal and after finishing their shopping for toiletries, were back in their apartment before midnight.

CHAPTER TWO

The novice agents decided to wait until tomorrow to review the case material and called it a night. The next morning Alice was awakened by noises in the kitchen and then a timid knock on her bedroom door. Since she was sleeping in the nude because of her oversight in obtaining night wear, she cracked the door and asked, "What's wrong?"

"There's nothing to make for breakfast. Let's go out to eat and then bring some groceries back with us."

"Okay, give me time to get dressed."

Later, while waiting on their breakfast order he asked, "I was afraid that you would be recognized as being from the Healing Guild because all the women members look alike. However, no one we've met seems to notice."

"Maybe people only look at the Red or Blue clothing and not the face, so when I'm in these clothes no one notices me except as a woman."

"A very beautiful woman I might add. Where did you come from?"

Alice's face heated in a flush before answering. "I'm from Dallas, how about you?"

"Baltimore. My exposure to life outside the Guild is very limited."

"The same. Even school was at the Guild. I wonder why they picked us for this task?"

"What were you doing when they transferred you here?"

"I was performing medical procedures, like most of the other Blues. How did you get all those muscles?"

"A hobby. I'm a Black Belt in Judo and I lift weights. While researching my Pearson ancestors I found they were proficient in Judo, so I tried it to see what the attraction was."

"What type of work were you doing?"

"I was making tests of my ability to read minds of people who were using key words. I'm the source of the information that someone is planning to attack the Guild for profit."

Alice looked at Aaron in surprise. "What's your effective range?"

"Global. The only clue as to the location of the individuals was that the readings were strong. What's your range?"

"I can read people anywhere in North America. However, from Dallas, anything further than the east or west coast is weak. You must be the strongest telepath we have."

"What's your strongest power?"

"Until now I thought telepathy was. Next is telekinesis. I can lift heavy weights, such as the cab we used yesterday."

"I'm probably more powerful than you then, and we are the top performers of the Guild. Whoops, looks like our food is arriving."

Alice looked at Aaron in speculation as they ate; twice she started to speak then stopped herself. After the second false start, Aaron said, "Get it off your chest."

You must have a plan, otherwise why start this department. You said the reading was strong, which means close to Baltimore. So why is our office here?

Aaron tasted her mental signature with pleasure and gave her a crooked smile. *We need training, which means we have to train ourselves. I'd rather do it away from our target area until I'm sure we can do this safely. I was thinking of picking a target that we could both receive a strong reading from, then triangulate the reading by moving apart and then separately move toward the target until we sight each other. That would indicate that our target was nearby.*

Alice's own taste of Aaron's mind glow caused her to tremble with desire. It was a powerful aphrodisiac that threatened to overwhelm her until, as a distraction, she pictured something that really disgusted her. She reached across the table and grabbed his hand. *Don't project your mind at me unless you want me to sexually attack you. It acts as a powerful aphrodisiac on me.*

"I'm sorry. I've never had that effect on other women I've mind talked with. This is terrible. How can we work together if I affect you that way?"

"Let's get our groceries and return to the apartment. Maybe I can block the worst of your effect on me."

After they returned to the apartment, Aaron put away the groceries while Alice considered different ways to block his mental effect on her. He sat at the kitchen bar with her and asked, "Any ideas?"

Alice stood and leaned over and sniffed his odor, which caused her to shudder. "I think I'm just attracted to you, even your smell elicits a response from me. I'm going to put up a partial mental block and when I point at you, mentally talk to me until I point at you again."

At her signal he began mentally talking to her until almost three minutes later she signed for him to stop. Alice placed her hand on his shoulder, and then flinched away. "Aaron, I could only open my block about a third before your attraction was more than I could resist. Do you have an attraction towards me at all?"

"More than any other woman I've met, but I can control myself. I don't understand what's going on here."

Suddenly another woman wearing clothing from a past century joined them. Alice grabbed Aaron's arm in a tight grip as they faced the woman who radiated love at them. The beautiful woman looked at them and shook her head in frustration. "You idiots, what you feel is love for each other. Alice, if you just admit that you love him, then the attraction you feel for him is manageable."

Aaron suddenly smiled and blurted, "You're Barbara Powers, the messenger angel of my ancestors!"

"Yes, you're both direct descendants of Angel Pearson, my niece. You were chosen to begin this defense against threats to the Healing Guild. As mates you will be a strong foe against the forces of evil. Don't fight your attraction for each other. We provided it to make you a stronger team. If you need me just say my name out loud."

Barbara left as silently as she arrived. Alice pulled Aaron into her embrace and looked into his eyes. "So this attraction between us was planned by God and we shouldn't fight it. I think we need to consummate our union for this to work properly. Do you agree?"

Yes, but first I want to kiss those lips that have been driving me crazy.

Alice suddenly kissed Aaron, who quickly joined her in eager ardor. When they broke apart for air, she grabbed his hand and drew him into her bedroom, where they quickly shed their clothing and Silks. They eagerly used their fingers to explore each other's bodies until they fell onto the bed and made passionate love. Being first time lovers they couldn't seem to get their fill of each other until finally they lay sated in each other's arms.

Alice murmured, "Oh, that was nice and you smell so good. I wonder how you taste?" Then she used her tongue to lick the skin over his abs.

"Do what you may, but I'm completely exhausted."

"If I feed you something do you think that'll help?"

"Rest, then food. Give me a break Alice."

"Oh, poor baby. Can I kiss it to make it feel better?"

"I think you broke it. Come give me a kiss and then I'll see if I can make it into the kitchen so I can watch you make us something to eat."

"Okay, but it better be something simple or we'll both starve."

How does this feel now? Are you able to cope?

Yes dear. I guess all I needed was some loving from you. I feel fine now.

You may have to help me out of bed; I think I pulled something.

Show me where it's at and I'll see if I can fix it.

Alice started massaging the muscles where Aaron indicated and he started making joyful noises as the muscles relaxed. After fifteen minutes of this treatment she helped him up and they made their way to the shower where they spent another twenty minutes under the hot spray of pulsating water. They each donned minimal clothing and made their way to the kitchen where they settled for corned beef on rye and milk. Alice asked, "Tell me about Barbara?"

"Our founders, Jackson Pearson and Jennifer Powers, were the parents of Angel Pearson. Barbara was the older sister of Jennifer and engaged to marry Jackson or Jack as he was known. Barbara was a budding artist and gave her self-portrait to Jack shortly before she died in a vehicle accident. She appeared to us as she looked in the portrait. After her death Jack was heartbroken and lost contact with the Powers family until he met Jennifer or Jenn as she was known, when she came to work as an Assistant U. S. Attorney in Kansas City. Jack was her supervisor and through a series of events they were married a week later. Apparently Jack and his family were protected by a Guardian Angel named Olivia and Barbara eventually arrived as a Messenger Angel."

"I wonder why I was never told this story of my history. So we are their direct descendants?"

"Yeah, that was over 200 years ago and a lot has changed since then, but apparently Barbara is still connected to our family. I wonder if Olivia is too."

"I'm still a little awed that we're part of God's plans to protect the Guild. I wonder if the Priestess is fully aware of His plan?"

Aaron chuckled. "How about us? I bet there's more that Barbara hasn't told us yet. Regardless, join me in my thoughts and I'll scan for someone we can use as a test target."

After a few minutes of concentration, he said, *there! This one is interesting. She's heading to work and thinking of Jack, a co-worker.*

Yes. She must live near here as I can feel her moving away from us in a westerly direction, Alice thought.

Can you continue to monitor her while we do other things, like get dressed and prepare to triangulate her position after she reaches her destination?

Yes. Aaron, I find this easier to do than before our mind merge. Do you think I've gained extra power from you?

Anything's possible. After this test run we'll do some experiments.

She seems to have stopped moving away. I would guess our target is about fifteen kilometers west of us. Do you agree?

Aaron pulled Alice toward him in a tight embrace and they

kissed passionately. She then gave him a quick kiss on the tip of his nose, saying, "Well, I didn't kill it after all. In fact it feels quite strong."

"Never mind. Work before play as the saying goes. Let's get dressed and don't forget your Silks. We need to get into the habit of wearing it when we go on a mission."

After dressing they met in the common room where Alice found Aaron looking at a city map of Kansas City. He pointed at their location and then checking the map's scale, estimated what was in a westerly direction fifteen kilometers away. Alice pointed at two locations three kilometers apart, north and south of the targets west line of travel.

"Why don't I take a robo cab to the south location and you take the north. When we get there I'll contact you mentally and we'll set a new vector toward our target. Agreed?"

He nodded and they kissed again before leaving the apartment. Alice thought, *who would have thought I would have found my mate and started a new career as an agent for the Guild this time last week.*

They each reached their initial location and set a new vector slightly west and toward each other's locations. They eventually left their cabs and walked less than two blocks before seeing each other a block apart. There was a large multi-storied building ahead of them housing a medical clinic. Aaron thought, *this must be where she works. Use your power to try to pinpoint where in the building she's located.*

They walked slowly toward each other and eventually stood together looking at its entrance. Alice said, "She's on the second floor about fifty meters from the front wall of the building. I know I didn't have that ability before!"

"I agree on her location. For this test, the mission is over. Okay, let's teleport back to our apartment."

"What! I can't do that! I've never even known anyone who could do that."

"It's simple. Picture our apartment's common room and just wish yourself there. But before we do that, let's get off the street where someone might see us and have a stroke seeing us disappear."

They entered the clinic and found an area with no one around.

Aaron took her hand and repeated his instructions then said, "On the count of three. One..two.."

"..three." Alice found she and Aaron were back in their apartment. She hugged him tightly and said, "That scared me so bad my knees are still knocking!"

"It looks like you have all my powers now and apparently at my strength levels. This is starting to look up for us. So you didn't know teleportation could be done?"

"No. How many people do you know who can do that?"

"Besides you and me, no one."

Alice looked at Aaron in surprise. "We're the only ones?"

"I guess we have a pretty exclusive club. How would you like to meet by mother?"

Alice's face paled at the thought of meeting her mother-in-law. "I can just hear her first words to me, how long have you known my son? She's going to think the worst of me when I say two days!"

Aaron hugged her and said, "It's not going to get any better the longer we wait. I'll mentally let her know we're coming while you gather two changes of clothing and toiletries. I saved a grocery bag that we can use to put our things in."

Fifteen minutes later they stood together in the common room. Aaron said, "Look into my mind and see the picture of where we want to go. Picture that image in your own mind paying close attention to the details. Now on my saying go, wish yourself there. G.."

"..o." They were standing in the room they had pictured in their minds. Alice sensed a presence behind them and turned to see a woman that looked almost identical to her own mother. Aaron said, "Mother, this is Alice Jackson, my mate."

"I hope to God that you're a Blue and not a Red. With my son I can never be sure what he is capable of."

"I'm beginning to believe that too. I'm sorry we haven't told you before, but we've only known each other two days. I'm still a little shook by this teleporting business."

"Aaron, Alice sit on the couch together and tell me what's been happening. Alice you can call me Joan."

Aaron and Alice took turns telling her of what occurred during the past two days, until Joan interrupted. "You say Barbara appeared. You mean our angel Barbara? I'm not aware of her appearing to any of us in over 200 years. Go on."

When their story was finished, Joan looked at the two proudly and with a little awe. "My, that's some story. The women always seem to feel the connection stronger than the men when they first meet their mates, but Alice you were really hit over the head with your reaction. I guess God wanted to be sure you noticed. Barbara's comment to you verifies that. Aaron, what are your plans?"

"May we stay here with you for a few days while we try and determine who these people are that pose a threat to the Guild."

"Yes, of course. Your father will be home shortly and I'm afraid you'll have to repeat your story. When's the last time you've eaten?"

"Too long ago."

"Alice come help me in the kitchen and tell me about yourself while we prepare something for our mates."

CHAPTER THREE

That evening after they retired to Aaron's old bedroom, Alice asked, "Does your twin sister have your powers?"

"No. I was considered a freak because of the extent of my powers. Mary has the same powers and strength as my parents. She's been mated three years and has a baby girl. Mother was beginning to worry that I'd never find my mate. She seems happy now that I've found you."

"Your father seems nice. What was it like growing up here in Baltimore?"

"I hardly ever left the compound until I started learning the Guild's history and discovered what part the old Johns Hopkins University and Hospital had in the lives of our ancestors. Our compound was built on their grounds and although the buildings are long gone, there is a monument to the earliest family members who studied here. I don't know how many generations of the family went through here, but it made enough of an impression that the northeast coast Guild Temple was established at this location."

"I guess we start on our task tomorrow, but I don't want to think about that tonight. I just want to have my mate wrapped in my arms and giving me his love."

"Yes dear, but try not to be so vocal as last time. I don't want my parents knocking on our door thinking I'm killing you."

"Oh Poo. If they do hear me it will be me crying out in ecstasy; however, I'll try to keep the volume down."

The next morning they were awakened by a knock on their bedroom door by Joan asking Alice if she wanted to help with breakfast. She quickly donned a T-shirt and shorts and left Aaron behind groaning about what time was it.

When Alice entered the kitchen Joan looked at her daughter-in-law with a small smile. Seeing the smile, Alice flushed saying, "I'm sorry. Were we too loud? I really tried to keep the sounds of our lovemaking to a minimum."

"Don't tell Aaron, but the sounds encouraged his father and me to follow your example. How does your family observe the mating ceremony?"

"After consummation the couple has one month to post notice of their mating bonding. Then members of the immediate families gather to celebrate their mating. Is that how it's done here?"

"Yes, but the male family hosts the gathering. Is that going to be a problem?"

"I don't think so, but I haven't told mother yet. I don't know how she's going to react to me mating with a man I've only known a few days. How would you have reacted if Mary had just told you that information?"

"Yes, I see your problem. Can I help in some way?"

"After breakfast Aaron and I may have to teleport to Dallas to notify my family. Hopefully, we'll be back before mid-day. What's your schedule?"

"I've already notified my supervisor that I'm taking the rest of the week off. Robert is still going to work as usual. Is it possible for you and Aaron to teleport me with you? I think I can help you with your mother."

They were both startled when Aaron answered, "I've never done it, but if I can carry a bag with us here, I'm sure we can."

Alice quickly went to her mate and kissed him. "I'll let my mother know we're coming with important news in about an hour. Is that okay?"

"Better make it two hours. We need to eat, clean up, change into appropriate clothing, and fix our faces," Joan said with a smile as she observed how in love they were.

Later, after everyone was ready and the target room firmly in

Aaron and Alice's minds, they both hugged Joan between them and teleported. They were startled by a loud scream as they arrived in Dallas. The three quickly gathered around Alice's mother who was recovering from the scare of her life.

"Alice don't ever do that again without telling me."

"But I did. We arrived almost to the minute I told you we were coming."

"I thought you were coming through the front door, not out of thin air!"

"Oh. I'm sorry mom. I guess I forgot to tell you I could teleport now."

"I hope that's not what the news was about."

"Mom, this is Aaron Pearson and his mom Joan. Aaron and I are mated. Aaron and Joan this is Rachel, my mother."

Rachel's mouth dropped open for a moment, then she appeared to gather her wits about her and started to examine her visitors. "Aaron, how old are you and where are you from?"

"Twenty-four and we're from Baltimore."

"You two met in Kansas City?"

"Yes."

"So you've known each other, what…three, four days?"

"About that. We were mated two days ago."

"That's not logical! That would take drugs or an act of God!"

Alice said, "It was the latter. When Aaron spoke to me mentally I was so overcome with longing for him that I couldn't block it out unless I shut him out completely. We thought our partnership was doomed before it began until the angel Barbara appeared and told us what we felt was love for each other and the overwhelming longing I felt for him would be contained when we mated. She was right, but I also received all his powers as well, including the ability to teleport."

Rachel looked at her daughter with tears in her eyes. "So you do love him?"

"With all my heart and soul."

Rachel hugged her daughter and then kissed her on her cheek. She then examined Aaron for a moment before saying, "You are a handsome devil. Do you love Alice?"

"Yes. I didn't know what I was missing until she came into my life."

"Joan, do you vouch for his character?"

"Yes. He's a handful, but he's of good character and soul. This was a shock for me too when they showed up in Baltimore yesterday. As the man's family we stand behind him and will host the gathering celebrating their mating."

"Very well, I will post the notice of their mating bonding. What was the date of the bonding?"

Aaron said, "August 14, 2318."

"Now, I want the full story of your meeting with Barbara. That meeting is historic for our families and perhaps the Guild."

Later, after they returned to Baltimore, Aaron and Alice returned to their bedroom where they both mind searched for anyone thinking about Guild members. Alice got the first hit and had Aaron follow her connection. The signal was strong and was from an individual speaking to another about how they were going to disable a Blue without causing serious harm. They immediately left the apartment using two robo cabs to begin their search. They only traveled five kilometers before stopping to determine their new vector. The signal was very strong for Aaron, less than one kilometer to his left and slightly ahead of his location, while Alice's target was about three kilometers to her right. Fifteen minutes later they were both standing before a two-story building with a company name of *Cramer Electronics*. There were three individuals now talking to each other and they were located at the rear of the second floor.

They entered the building looking for the office and discovered that the second floor was leased to *Costlow Consultants*. Rather than make direct contact, Aaron suggested they try the Cramer office for information on their tenant. When entering the office they faced a counter and could see that the business mainly hired young women. Alice mentally told Aaron, *you're the best person to handle these women.*

When several women saw Aaron standing at the counter it caused a foot race to see who would reach him first. Alice was standing beside Aaron at the counter, but the winner of the race had eyes only for him. Aaron smiled at the woman, who seemed to swoon before making a visible effort to collect herself and asked, "What can I do for you?"

"I'm doing a survey of two businesses sharing a small

building. What can you tell me about the business upstairs?"

"Oh, not much. They've only been there a little over a month and they keep to themselves. I've only seen three men go upstairs and they looked pretty rough, you now not who I'd want to meet on a dark street."

Aaron asked about their business and when finished he thanked the woman before they left the building. They teleported back to Aaron's bedroom where Alice asked, "Should we report our findings to Control before we take any further action?"

Aaron thought a few moments before nodding in agreement. "I don't see us doing anything other than direct action against them. I'll call Control and set up a meeting."

"Control wants us in her office ASAP. Are you ready?"

At her nod they teleported together into Control's office. Natalie jumped a little in her chair as we materialized. She swallowed an oath then glared at us. "You did that on purpose, didn't you?"

Alice said, "I'm sorry, I thought you were aware we could teleport."

"Well I wasn't aware, but I am now! Young wise crackers, trying to scare a woman out of ten years of her life. So report!"

Aaron didn't crack a smile as he reported what they had found. "We need instructions before we proceed further."

Natalie looked at them for several moments before her eyes opened in surprise. "You've bonded! I knew there was something different about you two, but I was distracted by you teleporting into my office. Alice you're much stronger too, so you must have acquired Aaron's powers when you mated. The Priestess needs to know this too. Now there are two of you, good, good, this is excellent. Go change into your Blues and I'll get you into to see the Priestess soon."

Ten minutes after changing they were ushered into the Priestess's chamber. She looked at them in surprise and then said, "It's true, you have mated. How is that possible! Aaron you didn't do anything despicable did you?"

Alice hid a smile behind her hand, then said. "When he first mentally spoke to me I was overwhelmed with what I thought was lust for him, but later when Barbara appeared she told us it was love and we needed to mate for this effect to be manageable."

"Barbara! You saw and spoke to the angel Barbara? Has she come back to your family after all these years?" The Priestess exclaimed with tears of happiness running down her cheeks.

She then asked, "Aaron, Natalie tells me Alice has obtained your powers. Is that true?"

"Yes, and in an effort for full disclosure, we both have the gift of healing as well."

"What! Aaron, I wasn't aware that you had that power. That makes you two the most powerful members of the Guild! Why did you hide that gift?"

"I was already considered a freak because of the powers I had. I was afraid you would make me a Red and I wouldn't fit there either."

"You're right, neither of you fit as a Red or a Blue. What color do you both like?"

Aaron said, "Black is too sinister, it would put fear into any Red or Blue who sees us. What do you think Alice?"

"No matter what color we choose it will have that effect. I like street clothes. When others see us they will have no idea who we are."

"I agree, we want to be undercover anyway, so that suits us best."

The Priestess smiled at them. "So be it. The secret will be easier to keep that way. Only your immediate family is to know of this power. Do you think they can keep this a secret?"

When they both agreed that their families could be trusted to keep their secret the Priestess said, "Continue to wear your Blues inside the building. Now as to your actions against these misguided fools, what do you think should be done?"

Aaron mentally consulted with his mate and they quickly agreed on a plan. Aaron said, "We think the best recourse is to plant a thought in their brains that they shouldn't plot against the Guild and its followers. Any time they hear or start to think about such a plot they lose that train of thought and if they persist they will black out. I know this is against our code of conduct, but our only other recourse is to eliminate them or do a mind wipe."

The Priestess looked at them in distress. "Tamper with there minds or kill them. Both options appear extreme to me. Natalie what are your thoughts?"

"I believe those are the only options available to us. I don't think you want to wait until they act and harm Guild members. Persuading them to leave us alone seems the less odious of our choices."

"Very well. After you perform this task do you think any follow up will be necessary?"

Alice answered, "No, my lady. We will bury the commands deep into their subconscious and they shouldn't even be aware of our tampering."

"Good. Now back to your conversation with God's Messenger Angel Barbara. Please tell me everything about her visit with you."

Aaron and Alice eventually teleported back to their bedroom in Baltimore. It was late in the afternoon and they decided to return to their targets' location early tomorrow. Alice followed Aaron out of the bedroom and they found his mother in the kitchen preparing a meal. Joan looked up at their entrance and asked, "Are you two home for the day?"

Aaron replied, "Yes Mother, we don't leave again until in the morning. What are you preparing? You don't have to go to a lot of effort for us."

"Alice can help me. Besides, I want to talk to her. It's been a little lonely without you and Mary underfoot."

CHAPTER FOUR

Later after dinner was finished, Aaron said, "I've got something important to tell you and you can't repeat it to anyone. Alice and I have the ability to heal by touch. We've discussed this with the Priestess and we are only able to disclose this to our immediate family. This information can't be allowed to get out."

Both Joan and Robert looked at their son in surprise and a little fear. Joan said, "So this is the real reason why you never made any close ties with your classmates or had any girlfriends. Are you going to be a Red now?"

"No, Reds are all women healers and I wouldn't fit. Alice and I are special cases. Apparently we are the most powerful members of the Guild, but because of our undercover assignments we were told to disguise ourselves as Blues whenever we report to our Control at the Guild. No one else can know of our healing ability."

Robert asked, "Son, what are you two doing for the Guild?"

"We are a special unit used to find and eliminate problems associated with the Guild."

Joan said, "That sounds to me like you're trouble shooters. Is this going to be dangerous?"

Alice said, "It can be, so we are planning our moves so that we watch each other's backs. We can always teleport out of a bad situation if we need to."

Joan looked at them and shook her head in admiration. "You two are following in the steps of our founders. Courageous and with little thought to the risks you're taking, all for the benefit of others. Watch out for each other, I don't want to lose either one of you."

The next morning over breakfast they discussed how to best face their targets. They finally settled on the direct approach. If all three were present when they arrived at the building, they would enter the room and freeze them in place, thus giving them ample time to work on them.

They teleported to the inside foyer of the Cramer Electronics Building, then after ensuring their targets were present, they climbed the stairs and tried the door, which was open. They found themselves in a small, unoccupied room with another door that was locked. Aaron pressed a buzzer labeled 'For Service', and they waited.

They could hear one set of footsteps approaching and a man opened the door and started to say something when he was hit by Aaron's freeze command. They squeezed around his body at the door and hurried inside. Two other men looked up at them as they entered the room and started to stand, when Alice's freeze command stopped them.

Aaron released the first man frozen in the doorway and replaced it with a follow me command as they walked together to where the other two men were, then froze him in place again. The agents started a search of the room for any documents or a comp that would give them more information on this group and if they were affiliated with others.

Alice sat down before a comp that was running and started searching for files that might help them, while Aaron leafed through several folders of paper files. They had been searching for about thirty minutes when a beeping sound of a personal com was heard. Alice quickly found the devise on one of the men and saw a text message displayed, which she showed Aaron.

It read, *Meet at location A at 2 p.m. for party.* Alice said, "I'll get from this guy where A is and who's the party."

While Alice was combing through the man's memories, Aaron resumed his inspection of the paper records. Finally satisfied that there was nothing pertaining to other parties or the text message, he turned to the comp and resumed what Alice had started. Later, satisfied that there was nothing on the comp that wouldn't take hours to find, he started cleaning the minds of the other two men.

An hour later he looked up and found that Alice was finished with her man. He said, "What did you find?"

"A is the corner of Broadway and Park and the party is two Blues who habitually go to a coffee shop at that time. They planned a snatch and grab on them using a stolen city vehicle and are to deliver them to a warehouse on River Road and Falstaff."

Aaron thought through several ways they could handle this. "Alice, we could do the pickup and delivery if you have a mental picture of the warehouse. If the two Blues have weak powers, we can return them to their residence and handle this ourselves. The problem is we don't know how many people are at the warehouse."

"Can't we determine that when we get there and if the odds are too bad we can do something else?"

"Okay, I'm going to call Control and see what she thinks."

After making the mental call, he looked at Alice and asked, "Did you hear what she said?"

Alice grinned. "Control seemed a little upset. I didn't catch all of it, we meet the others where?"

"A block from the target at 2:15 p.m., and we are in charge of the operation. These guys here won't wake up until way after the operation. I'm hungry, how about you?"

"Let's take your mother out for lunch, but we shouldn't tell her anything about what we're doing this afternoon. It might scare her."

* * *

Aaron and Alice used the city truck they found at the rear of the Cramer Building and arrived a few minutes before the appointed time. They at first thought they were the first to arrive; however, as soon as they left their vehicle six men and women stepped out from where they were hiding between buildings. None of them were wearing their blue uniforms, which made the group nondescript except for their actions.

Aaron asked the group, "Has anyone seen any activity?"

A woman replied, "Not while we've been here. What's the

plan?"

Alice said, "I count seven other minds in the building and they are not aware we're here yet."

"I plan on driving up to the delivery door and honk. Hopefully, they will open the door for us to drive in and everyone inside should then be frozen in place. Anyone not able to do that?"

The woman said, "We're ready when you are."

Aaron said, "Okay, everyone get in the truck and let's get this done."

Everything worked as planned and they were soon in the building. As soon as the vehicle stopped, everyone exploded out of it and started freezing in place everyone in sight. Aaron counted the targets and found two missing. He mentally told his team, *we've got two missing men, be careful in your search.*

Alice pointed to an overhead group of rooms at the rear of the building. "They're in the center office and are armed."

Aaron said, "Alice, you teleport to the right side of that room and I'll take the left. Let's do it on two, one…"

"…two." They were both in place and Alice thought, *I can see through their eyes. They are sitting on the floor behind a desk and both have a hand weapon.*

Aaron responded, *you take the one on your side and I'll take the other. Make their weapons too hot to hold. Do it now!*

Nothing happened for about five seconds and then there were screams followed by the noise of two objects hitting the floor. Aaron and Alice quickly entered the room and froze the two in place. Aaron scanned the area for any others and found nothing, so he called for help to move these two down with the others.

The woman, who appeared to lead the other Blues said, "My name is Blaise Thompson. Do you need us for anything else?"

"Yes, would your people stack all but these last two in the vehicle with a twelve hour wake up. I'm going to leave this truck where the police can find it. By the way, I'm Aaron Pearson and this is my mate, Alice Jackson."

"You two are scary powerful. I didn't even know teleportation was possible. I was told to give you my name in case you need help here in the future."

Aaron and Alice thanked everyone for their help before they departed, leaving them with the task of combing the minds and bodies for additional information. After searching through the memories of the two they found upstairs they concluded they had contained the source from this threat. It was apparent they had no idea of the source of the Guild's powers or how powerful the Guild members were. The two Blues they were planning on abducting might have been killed, but it was possible they could have handled this group themselves.

The five in the truck were hired muscle and were to be paid off when they had possession of the Blues. These men Aaron and Alice only wiped their memories on whom they were trying to abduct. The two leaders' memories were selectively wiped as well. Enough remained that would tie them to the attempted abduction, but would be vague as to who was their target.

Satisfied they had done all they needed to do, they drove to a nearby police station; wiped down any surface they may have touched and placed the two leaders in the truck's cab. They made sure these men's fingerprints were on the steering wheel and other surfaces. They then com'd the police reporting where the stolen city truck could be found before teleporting back to Aaron's family home.

Aaron looked at Alice for a moment before taking her into his arms and giving her a long passionate kiss. Alice finally broke the kiss and nibbled on his earlobe before saying, "Honey, that was exciting, what's next?"

"We report to Control. Would you let her know we're coming in about fifteen minutes?"

"There, it's done. I need to use the bathroom too, so hurry."

They teleported to Kansas City almost to the minute of their appointment and Natalie looked up from her work and smiled when they arrived in her office. "I take it you and your team took care of the problem?"

Aaron said, "It went well. Do you have a quick response team at all our locations?"

"No, just in the States."

Alice said, "Blaise Thompson's team were first rate. I hope the others we have to use are as good."

"Okay, tell me what you did since I saw you last."

When they finished their debriefing, Natalie checked the Baltimore News download for anything on the truck full of unconscious people. "Well, according to this there is confusion of what happened to the men in the stolen city truck, but it was obvious they were responsible for stealing it and someone in their group told the police about an attempted kidnapping that went bad, which they then traced to two locations that were used. They should be charged for the stolen truck at the very least."

Aaron said, "What have you planned for us next?"

"Use your powers to uncover anything that might harm the Guild, either physically or our reputation. I'll pass this information that you provided to the Priestess. You are on your own until you find something else or we contact you."

Alice said, "We have a mating ceremony to prepare for, so give us ten days if possible."

Natalie suddenly looked thoughtful. "I'd like to attend too. Let me know where and when."

Alice paled. "You don't intend for the Priestess to be present do you?"

"No, not in person, but maybe by vid. Is that going to be a problem?"

Aaron said, "Won't that bring us more attention than we should have considering what we do?"

"Mmm. Perhaps you're right, but if I'm the only one who comes you can pass me off as a distant cousin, which I am."

Aaron said, "Okay, when we have our plans finalized we'll let you know. So far all we know is the city - Baltimore. My parents are hosting the ceremony."

Aaron and Alice teleported back to Baltimore to find Aaron's mother watching the vid. Joan looked up when they arrived and said, "They've charged a bunch of men for stealing a city truck. What would anyone want to do something stupid like that?"

Aaron said, "Mom, let's start planning for the Mating Ceremony. We have some free time now, which may change soon. Oh, and Natalie Bertram, who handles the Priestess's affairs wants to attend as well."

Joan slowly turned to her son and said, "What does that mean? Is this going to turn into a Guild Ceremony with the Priestess attending?"

"We're not certain at this point. Natalie mentioned that it's possible the Priestess may attend via a vid hookup, but for now it's just Natalie. How many people are you thinking of inviting?"

"I've talked to Alice's mother and she's bringing ten family members. Since we're local I think we'll have at least twenty representing our family. The Temple meeting hall holds 500, so everybody who wants to come should fit. The reception will be here afterwards. If either of you wants to make a change now is the time."

Alice reluctantly said, "I've got a bad feeling about what happens if the Priestess is involved. Even if she's not here in person I'm afraid the hall is not going hold everyone, and forget about holding the reception here."

Joan shrugged her shoulders and said, "The only thing we can change is the where we hold the reception. I'm going to reserve the gym for our reception and if it's certain that the Priestess is involved in any way I'll triple our caterer's order."

Alice said, "If the Priestess is involved, I'm sure my family will be anxious to share in the expenses."

"I know my dear, but it's really our family's obligation. We'll pass the hat if it comes to that. Do you two have a date in mind?"

Alice said, "We want it soon, so how about this Saturday morning. Will five days be enough time to prepare?"

"Alice, why don't you teleport home and discuss this with your mother before we make reservations."

"Okay. Aaron don't go anywhere, I'll be back soon." Alice gave him a lingering kiss and disappeared with a soft pop.

Aaron wistfully looked at the empty space where she had stood for a few moments, then sighed. "I miss her already. Is this what love is?"

"Yes dear. Even now I sometimes ache when your father isn't with me. I was really worried that you wouldn't find your mate, now I worry that this new job is too risky. I don't want to lose either one of you!"

"Mom, don't worry. With the powers we have I can't think of anyone being able to sneak up on both of us."

"Maybe so, just don't get over confident."

Alice arrived in her Dallas home to find her mother looking through her files of still pictures of her children. She stood watching her for a few minutes until finally she started to clear her throat to let her mother know that she wasn't alone, when her mother said, "Alice, come here a moment. I want to show you something."

"How did you know I was here?"

"I could sense your mind glow. It's so much stronger now than before you bonded with Aaron. Look at this picture of you when you graduated from medical school."

Alice leaned over and looked at the 3-D image. "I look so innocent and full of myself."

"Yes, you never lacked self-confidence, even now with what you are doing with Aaron. Not many of us would even attempt to do what you have accomplished."

"We're going to try to have the Mating Ceremony this Saturday morning. Is this going to be a problem?"

"I've checked the cost of a shuttle or the bullet train. The train is cheaper by half but takes three hours longer. If we leave early enough on the train we will be there on time, assuming it's after nine a.m."

"What should I wear? Grace wore a white dress for hers, but I don't have anything like that."

Rachel smiled at her concern. "Your sister brought over her white dress, so let's see if it will fit you."

CHAPTER FIVE

Later, Alice teleported back to Baltimore with a white dress carefully held in her arms. Joan's face showed her joy when she saw the dress. "Let's go to my room. I've got to see you in that dress."

Alice kissed her mate and hurried after Joan. "What's the big deal about that dress," he wondered aloud.

After Alice changed into the dress, Joan carefully touched the material and asked, "Do you know how old this dress is?"

"Mom told me it's been in the family for at least 150 years. It's got handmade lace around the bodice and sleeves. She told me it's now my responsibility to care for it until my last daughter marries, then she pass's it on."

"Our family dress went to my sister and reportedly it was even older than this one is. However, yours is prettier and the skirt is a little longer. It almost touches the floor. Have you researched the history of the white dress used in the Mating Ceremony?"

"No, but I know it goes back a long time."

"The white dress began before the Seventeenth Century and was called a Wedding Dress, used when a couple got married. The color represented purity and was supposed to show that the bride was a virgin. Later, that feature was played down, as few virgin brides were married. However, today our Mating Ceremony took the place of what was formally called a wedding, but we still use a white dress during the ceremony."

"What did a wedding dress look like, do you have an image?"

"Yes. I've got one over here." Joan showed Alice the 3-D image. Her eyes got big in fascination.

"It's beautiful, but how did she walk with skirts that full and long?"

"Obviously, the dress style changed over the years. However, the bride still values wearing the white dress, the older it is the better."

After changing out of the white dress, Alice returned to where Aaron was drinking coffee at the kitchen table. Before sitting beside him she fixed herself a cup of dark chocolate cocoa. She sat close enough to her mate that they touched shoulders and sighed as she took a first sip of her hot drink. "Ahh, this tastes so good. How can you stand that coffee?"

Aaron placed his arm around her waist and pulled her closer to him. "Did you get everything arranged in Dallas to your satisfaction?"

"Yes, plans are for them to take the bullet train here to arrive Saturday morning. We need to have the ceremony at eleven a.m. or later and we better get that arranged and the reception place reserved, as time is short."

The day of the Mating Ceremony arrived and true to Natalie's prediction the High Priestess was going to make a vid appearance after the ceremony. The Temple Auditorium was packed to overflowing, but Alice and Aaron didn't seem concerned as they were caught in a love trance as they gazed at each other during the ceremony.

At the ceremony's end they kissed passionately for a long moment, then seemed to realize where they were as they gave each other an embarrassed smile, then holding hands they bowed to the audience, who responded with loud applause.

The lights dimmed as a large vid screen dropped behind the pair on the stage. An image of the High Priestess appeared on the screen and she appeared to smile at the mated pair standing before her. "Congratulations on your Mating Aaron Pearson and Alice Jackson. Your joining was partially arranged by the angel Barbara who has not shown herself in over 250 years until recently when she appeared to these lucky individuals. I foresee a new emergence of Angels guiding us toward goals we can only guess at today. Give these two your blessing and help as needed."

The lights brightened as the vid screen rose. The audience went wild with applause and shouts of joy until they quieted when Aaron raised his hand. He then repeated the story of their experience with the angel Barbara. When he finished, the audience was struck speechless in wonder and awe as they realized the stories of angels they were raised on were real and happening again. They fell to their knees and prayed to God. When they began to regain their feet Alice invited everyone to the gym for their reception.

Later, after the reception was over and they were back in Aaron's family apartment, they could begin to comprehend what they had experienced. The reception line led from the auditorium to the gym and after seeing the crowd the caterer called for more food. Many of the people wanted to touch the hands of the pair obviously blessed by God, to have had an angel influence their union. The reception lasted four hours and only ended when the food was exhausted.

The family heads raised their wine glasses to there recently mated offspring and wished them success in their union and future endeavors. Joan Pearson and Rachel Jackson then toasted each other's families as they were now joined together by the Bonding. Eventually, everyone left but those who lived in the apartment.

Aaron and Alice sat with his parents at the kitchen table drinking hot coffee and cocoa recalling humorous occurrences they remembered from their hectic day. Aaron said, "My favorite was when Natalie Bertram was hit upon by Uncle Peter. I thought she was going to pop him in the mouth, but instead she kissed him on the cheek and winked at Alice. What was that about?"

Alice blushed and put her hand to her mouth to hide a laugh. "I put him up to it as a joke, but she must of read his mind. I guess I better be careful around her for a while because she knows I was behind the joke."

Aaron said in exasperation, "You are playing with fire when you play jokes on your boss. She has so many different ways of getting back at you."

"If I'm reading her correctly, she will try to pay me back in a like kind of joke. It's just harmless joking around."

"Mom, do we have jokers in our family?"

"Most of the women like to play jokes, it's the men who don't have a sense of humor."

Alice smiled at Aaron and gave him a wink. "Oh he's funny. He just doesn't know it most of the time."

Aaron grabbed at her and she quickly ran out of the room toward their bedroom with him close behind. Robert smiled ruefully at his mate and shook his head sadly. "What are we doing wrong? How come the young have all the fun?"

Joan got up from her chair and sat in his lap. "Oh, I still have some fun left in me, how about you?"

The next day Aaron and Alice sat together on the sofa and let their minds troll through the thoughts of others in search of anything to do with the Guild. It took practice but they were soon able to disregard everything else being thought except for key words. They took a break for lunch and Alice prepared sandwiches since both of Aaron's parents were working.

She asked her mate, "Did you have any discussions about our pay since we aren't in the Guild's normal structure any longer?"

"I assume we charge anything we need. Remember we have an unlimited chit."

"I know. It just seems like such a loose arrangement."

"Remember we have Natalie as our oversight. If she thinks a charge is excessive I'm sure she will let us know. Actually I'm sure everyone else in the Guild would like to have our arrangement."

"Okay, I give up. Do we go back to our apartment in Kansas City?"

"Yeah, but let's wait until tonight or tomorrow. I want to say goodbye to my parents before we leave."

That afternoon Aaron discovered someone who was thinking of the Guild in a threatening way. He told Alice to follow his thoughts to the person he was listening to. She said, "I'm reading it too. It is of medium strength coming from west-southwest of our location. Do you agree?"

"Yes. When my parents come home let's say our goodbyes and teleport to our Kansas City apartment. We can take another reading from that location before deciding what to do next."

Later, the couple said their goodbyes to Aaron's parents and was soon in Kansas City. They centered themselves and quickly found the mind they were searching for. It was a much stronger strength and was located southwest of their present location. Alice said, "The person is only about twenty kilometers from us, which is in Kansas. Let's eat out somewhere in the general location of our source. You go first and find a restaurant and we'll try to triangulate the signal, between your location and here."

Aaron agreed and took a robo cab to a location near the suspected source. Once there he mentally told Alice he was ready. She replied, *I've got a fix from here. Give me a visual of where you are and I'll join you with the map.*

They were soon standing together in an empty hallway of a restaurant. Aaron pointed inside. "Let's get a table and plot where this person is located."

Once seated, Alice asked, "What's the specialty here?"

Aaron handed her a menu and smiled. "Bar-b-que, what else."

He then spread the map out, found his location, turned the map to align with North and drew a line until it intersected with Alice's line. "Well, that's close, less than kilometer from here. When we leave here we'll take a cab to find the source."

They had just been served their meal when Alice looked at Aaron and said, "The source is moving, do you sense it?"

"Yes, it's getting closer to us."

The two picked at their food as their source kept getting closer, until fifteen minutes later they recognized the mental signature of their source requesting a table for two. They watched, as the woman was seated two tables away. She was with an older woman who was her mother according to her mental thoughts.

After the two ordered, the women began a quiet but heated argument about the daughter's relationship with a Blue, whose name was Wesley Parks. The source was Judy Simmons and her mother was Grace Simmons. Apparently, Wesley was reluctant to commit to a union with Judy because of her aversion to his telepathic powers. Judy liked the idea of a Blue for a mate because of its social status, but felt a deep revulsion for his ability to know her every thought. Grace was trying to change her daughter's mind because of the higher social status she would have if she mated with a Blue.

The two eavesdroppers knew from Judy's mindset that this

fear was too powerful for logic to work and the mating wouldn't happen. Judy's love for Wesley was turning to hate because of his powers. Aaron and Alice could feel Judy's frustration grow to a point she loudly whispered at her mother, "Shut up! Just shut up about Wesley! It's over between the two of us. He told me yesterday because of my fears we could never be mated. So that's it."

Alice looked at Aaron. *I believe that takes care of the potential problem from this source. What now?*

Let's finish our fine meal and try to avoid the emotional turmoil over there until we teleport back to our apartment.

The next morning Alice awoke to find herself wrapped in the arms of her mate. She smiled at the memory of their lovemaking after returning from the restaurant last night. She sniffed the smell of his musk from his body. It smelled so good that she used her tongue to taste him, then she nuzzled and softly bit him until he finally awoke and they made love again, slowly at first, then more urgently as their passion peaked.

Later, sated and relaxed in each other's arms, Aaron asked his mate if she was happy. Alice stretched like a big feline and kissed her mate. "Oh yes. We make good love together. Come, let's take a shower and I'll try to get you up for another run."

Alice crawled lazily out of bed and slowly walked toward the bathroom with Aaron only a step behind her.

CHAPTER SIX

Aaron and Alice were in their second week of scanning for any mental thoughts regarding the Guild when Aaron got a partial thought that might be something they should follow up on. He told Alice where to concentrate her efforts and they were both rewarded with a full thought that seemed to be part of a conversation with someone else.

The signal was weaker than it should be for anyone in the continental United States and appeared to be east of their location. After listening to the one-sided conversation for several minutes, they were sure they needed to discover more of what they were planning. It was also unusual they couldn't hear the other side of the conversation unless a personal com was being used.

Aaron decided he should teleport to Baltimore and then try to triangulate the target between the two of them. When he arrived in Baltimore they compared angles and found they were the same, which meant the target was in either England or Europe. Alice joined Aaron and they decided one of them would travel to Madrid to get a better angle between there and Baltimore.

They both went to the Baltimore Guild Temple and obtained Guild Embassy Passports, which allowed them unlimited access to any country having a Guild Temple. They flipped a good luck token Aaron carried with him and Alice won. She would travel to

Madrid and would inform Aaron of the new angle.

The Temple furnished her with a set of Blues to wear, and an Embassy Case to complete the disguise. Her shuttle left Baltimore less than two hours later. This was Alice's first international trip and she was a little anxious about what awaited her.

After clearing customs in short order because of her Embassy identity, she stopped at the airport café and ordered a hot tea while searching for the target's mental glow. Finding it she informed Aaron of her angle. He soon responded, *it's coming from London. Teleport back here and we'll prepare ourselves for the trip to London.*

When Alice arrived back in Baltimore, Aaron said, "We don't know how long we're going to be in London so let's each pack a bag and we'll dress in Blues and go as emissaries of the Guild. The next shuttle flight to London leaves in two hours, so we better hurry."

Three hours later Aaron was in the middle of London were he felt for the familiar mind glow he was seeking. He found it and compared it to the reading Alice gave him from her location. *Alice it looks like our target is about fifteen kilometers northwest of my location. Teleport to my location when you have a clear reading of my surroundings.*

When Alice arrived at his location she remarked, "Whew, some of these buildings are really old. What's the plan?"

"Before we find a hotel, let's stash our bags somewhere. We may not need to stay overnight if this doesn't pan out as a threat."

"We can leave them at that hotel over there. Tip the bellman to watch them for us until we check in."

They were soon in a robo cab heading toward their target. The map they were using showed the area as primarily residential. The cab was approaching several high-rise apartment buildings when Alice told it to stop at the nearest building on the left. They left the cab and entered the building's lobby and tried to eavesdrop on their target's thoughts.

After about ten minutes they left the building and started walking toward a covered transport station not far from the building. Finding themselves alone they teleported to the hotel where they left their bags. They checked in and it wasn't long before they were inside a suite the hotel had discounted because they were Guild Diplomats.

Aaron said, "Our target was thinking of a meet tonight, but we don't know the time. There was definitely malaise in the target's thoughts, but so far we don't know what they plan on doing."

They changed into street clothes and were monitoring the thoughts of their target. Because they were fearful the individual would detect a mind probe, they limited themselves to just reading the person's surface thoughts. The agents lucked out when the target received a com call changing the time and meeting place.

The pair could now take a robo cab to the meeting place without worrying about the target detecting their tail. Aaron and Alice ate a meal while continuing to monitor their target. Later, when leaving the hotel early so they would arrive at least an hour before the meet time, the two discovered London's uncertain weather had turned against them. A steady light rain was falling as they stepped outside and took a robo cab.

When they reached their destination they found a place to watch the building partially sheltered from the rain, but after a few minutes of discomfort Alice placed a force field over them, as the rain was becoming an annoyance. The night was dark and the nearest streetlight cast them in deep shadow, making them impossible to see from the building they were watching.

They were sure they were the first to arrive after finding no other mind glows nearby, and settled in to wait for the others. Twenty minutes later the first person arrived on foot and before entering the building, he looked around the area to see if anyone was watching. Seeing no one he entered and there was soon a light showing from a window on the second floor.

Searching his surface thoughts they discovered the man was excited and apprehensive about the coming meeting. He was fearful of someone named Anthony, who he considered very dangerous. Ten minutes later two people arrived by robo cab, a man and a woman, who immediately entered the building and joined the man they addressed as Jasper. The new arrivals were Ralph and Rosemary, and one of these was the initial target who they eventually learned was Ralph.

They were all waiting on Anthony's arrival, apparently their leader who they all feared. The last arrival soon joined them and after greetings they got down to the reason for their gathering.

Anthony outlined what each person's responsibility in the plot was and when the action would take place. The malice in Anthony's thoughts was evident as he told Jasper where to place the explosives inside the Guild Temple at noon tomorrow, set with a two hour timer. His glee was apparent as he visualized the Temple collapsing on everyone inside.

Deciding they had heard enough, Aaron and Alice used the visual clues from the occupants to teleport into the room, where they rendered the conspirators unconscious.

Aaron then mentally reported to Control. *Control, Alice and I have stopped a conspiracy to plant a bomb in the London Guild Temple and we need you to send a response team to our location.* He then gave her their address.

Control asked a few questions, then said, *check back with me in ten minutes, as I don't have your range in telepathy.* While they waited they did a deep mind scan of Anthony and the others making sure there were no other conspirators and finding where the explosives were stored in another room of this building.

Aaron then mentally checked back with Control. *Control, what's the situation with London?*

I told them of their problem and they are sending a team to your location. Check with Jason Briggs and let him know what to expect. Report to me here when everything is settled.

Alice kissed Aaron on the cheek and said, "Not even a congrat's on a job well done?"

"Maybe Control will give us a pat on the back when we report to her later."

"Do you want to check in with Jason or let me do it?"

"Go ahead and do it while I check and make sure the explosives are really here."

Jason Briggs can you hear me?

Yes, is this Aaron or Alice?

This is Alice. Aaron is checking to make sure the explosives are here and their condition. We have four people we have rendered unconscious and have performed deep mind scans on.

Would you open the front door for us, we'll be there in about ten minutes?

Sure, no problem. We're on the second floor.

Alice checked the condition of their captives and was thinking of looking for Aaron, when he returned. "There you are. I was just going to check on you."

"They have enough explosives to level this whole block."

"The London team will be here shortly and I need to let them inside. I just checked on these peoples' condition and they appear okay. See you in a few."

Alice could hear the arriving crew's mental thoughts as soon as she opened her mind to them, but it was another five minutes before they arrived. Alice smiled at them as they entered the building and followed her upstairs to where the four captives were.

Jason Briggs said, "Would you go over again what you did and how you learned about their plans."

Aaron explained, "We are a special department formed by the High Priestess to hunt for any mental thoughts that would present a threat to the Guild. We traced the thoughts of Ralph, the man with the red hair, to London. When we got here and found where he lived, we began closely monitoring his thoughts and determined there was a change in their plans for a meeting tonight. We got here early and monitored the people as they arrived. Anthony Richards, the man wearing a suit coat with a red vest, is the leader. When we overheard their plans to place a bomb in the temple tomorrow, set to explode two hours later, we teleported here and rendered them unconscious. You know the rest."

"Where are the explosives?"

"Follow me and I'll show you. There's enough there to more than bring down the temple. I wonder where they got it?"

When they reached the explosives Jason's voice became tense, "Why, this is military grade CX12. I may need your help in determining where they got access to this."

"Let's have another go at Anthony. He should know the source."

Returning to the room where the others were, Aaron dragged a chair close to Anthony and sat down, concentrating on probing his mind for thoughts relating to his acquisition of the explosives. After another ten minutes Aaron eased back in his chair and smiled at Jason.

"He got it from Sgt. Trevor Horn of the Queen's Guard. Apparently he didn't do it for money, but because he agreed with their cause and is the brother-in-law of Anthony. The Reds turned down Anthony's sister for a cure of her illness and she died before her appointment with the Blues. They blame the Guild for her death and that's the primary reason for their actions."

Jason frowned. "We need to make sure Sgt. Horn didn't have help with getting the explosives to Anthony, but we don't need you for that."

Aaron shook Jason's hand. "Well, I guess we're done here. The Priestess will want a report on the death of Anthony's sister and the steps taken to avoid this happening again if fault occurred by not following procedures. In addition, send a report on the disposition of the parties involved."

Aaron and Alice teleported to their hotel room and because of the late hour they decided to spend the night there before returning to Kansas City in the morning. Neither of them had ever stayed at such a luxurious hotel before and was enjoying themselves as they sampled the good life. After making passionate love in the soft king sized bed they fell asleep in each other's arms.

The next morning they ordered breakfast delivered to their room and showered together in a full body shower followed by a warm air dryer, instead of towels. After breakfast they teleported to Control's office, but not before they informed her they were on their way.

Natalie looked up at their arrival and smiled. "You look refreshed and happy. Tell me what you found in London and how you handled it."

When they finished their report, Natalie asked, "It's odd that the patient died before the Blues' appointment. If she was that close to death, then the Reds should have acted. I'm interested in the report from London in that regard. Until we get their report you two are dismissed."

Aaron and Alice teleported to their apartment and checked to see if they needed to shop for groceries; however, before starting that task they each mentally contacted their parents to let them know they were back in Kansas City after completing an assignment.

They were in their apartment mentally searching for leads when they received a summons from Control to report to her wearing their Blues. When Aaron and Alice arrived, Natalie checked them over before telling them the Priestess wanted to question them about their last assignment.

Fifteen minutes later they were standing before the Priestess. She smiled at them and congratulated them on a job well done. Then she said, "I've received London's report on what you discovered there and their report differs from yours on the death of Anthony's sister, who they report is Allison Horn. They report that Allison died before being treated by the Reds. Since you performed a deep mind scan on Anthony that revealed a different story, a story he believed to be true, we need to verify London's story. Natalie will provide each of you with a pin that tells everyone in the Guild that you are my personal representative, which should get you all the support you need. You will also have written authorization if they refuse to cooperate. Let Natalie know if you have any problems."

Aaron said, "What happened to the conspirators?"

"They will be of no help to you as they all have had a mind wipe for the period involved."

Alice grimaced, "That makes it convenient for them."

"Yes, but I don't think they have knowledge of your abilities. If there is wrong doing in London I want to know the full story."

They returned to Control's office where Natalie gave them the promised pins and documentation. "When you get to the London Temple the person you should first seek is Mary Ann Hicks. She is the head of security for the Temple."

"What if they stonewall me and refuse to cooperate?"

"We'll take it one step at a time. These pins have only been issued twice before. They are angels, in honor of our original member, Angel Pearson."

Aaron and Alice teleported back to their apartment and packed for a week, not knowing how long they would be gone. They then teleported to the front steps of the London Temple.

The pair was soon shown into the office of Mary Ann Hicks, Head of Security. After introductions were made Aaron handed Hicks their documentation. Hicks read the letter and then looked up at them. "You are the two who captured that group who wanted to blow up our Temple. What do you want from me?"

"Who prepared the report to the Priestess concerning the death of Allison Horn?"

"What report?"

Aaron and Alice looked at each other for a moment before Alice said, "How could a report that was addressed to the head of the Guild leave this Temple and not go through your office, especially if it involved the death of a patient? Who has the authority to bypass you?"

"Only the administrator, Lauren McCormick, has that authority," Hicks said with dawning awareness of trouble looming before her.

Aaron said, "We need to see her immediately and we want you to remain with us as we continue this investigation."

Hicks used her com to call the Administrator's office and talked to McCormick's secretary. When told McCormick was busy, Hicks told her this was an emergency and she needed to speak to her now. Less than a minute later, they heard McCormick say with a plainly irritated voice, "What is it Hicks, I'm busy here?"

"Representatives from the Priestess are here asking about a report sent by you regarding the death of Allison Horn and they want to speak to you now."

There was a lengthy silence before McCormick said, "I'm busy now, and they will have to wait."

Hicks replied, "You better get down here now or they'll come after you!"

"Oh, very well. I'll need another half hour to finish up here."

"Now! Get down here now or I'll send someone for you."

"Crap!" Then there was the sound of desk doors slamming.

Aaron concentrated until he found the administrator and placed a freeze on her ability to move. He then turned to Hicks and tensely said, "Get someone from your staff and we'll follow you to her office."

McCormick's secretary looked up in surprise at their arrival. Hicks asked, "She still in there?"

At the secretary's nod, they opened the door and found McCormick frozen in place with a comp chip in her hand. Hicks took the chip from McCormick's fingers and handed it to Aaron, "You are probably looking for this."

Aaron looked through the file on McCormick's comp while Alice scanned the administrator's memories. Aaron made a paper copy of the file and handed it to Hicks. "Apparently, McCormick was charging a fee for admission to Red treatments. McCormick is not one of us, why is that?"

"A quirk in English Law requires an administrator of medical facilities to have special training. Rather than send a Blue back to school for this training, we hired someone from outside the Guild."

Alice said, "My scan of McCormick revealed she had rewritten the admission procedures so that she reviewed all applications for approval. She put the bite on those she thought could pay her the fee she demanded. However, Allison Horn didn't have the ability to pay and during the extended negotiations she died. McCormick predated the refusal of Red treatment and the appointment for Blue treatment."

Hicks said, "How long has this been going on?"

"About a year. McCormick has a gambling problem and she needed these funds. I'm going to recommend that the administrator have no say in appointments and that the position be a member of the Guild. I'm also going to recommend that your office have oversight of all Temple operations."

"What do you want me to do with McCormick?"

"The Priestess will make that determination after we report back our findings. Keep her under confinement until that time. There, I've released her from my hold command."

Aaron and Alice then teleported to outside Control's office door, once inside the outer office they asked her secretary to speak to Natalie, and were soon ushered inside. Control looked at them and said, "Back so soon? I expected you to take longer."

"Security head Mary Ann Hicks was very helpful," and then proceeded to report their findings and recommendations.

CHAPTER SEVEN

Natalie looked at her two operatives with satisfaction. "I'm proud of you two. You have exceeded my expectations and I'll consider your recommendations. The Priestess will determine what actions to take and will inform London on what changes to make. You may take a day off and recharge before resuming your work."

They teleported back to their apartment and gathered their dirty clothes to run through the cleaner. Fifteen minutes later they were finished and on the couch in each other's arms watching a love story on the vid. Neither of them was aware when they fell asleep, but they lay together several hours before they woke.

Alice was the first to awake and her first thought was, *we must have used our energy reserves up by our frequent teleportation's today.* She gave her mate a kiss and went looking for energy bars. When she returned Aaron was sitting up on the couch and asked, "Alice what's wrong with me? I feel weak."

"I think we did too many teleportation's today. Here, eat this energy bar and then we'll go get some real food."

Later, after returning to their apartment they attempted to gage their energy levels. Aaron and Alice each thought they had more energy than before they ate, but not as much as they usually had. They agreed to curtail teleportation's until at least another nights rest.

They returned to the couch and replayed the vid they had fallen asleep watching. Alice made herself comfortable in Aaron's arms, but sleep was not what interrupted their viewing this time. Alice suddenly became incredibly horny and as her sexual desire for her mate increased, she became aware that Aaron was responding in like to her mental urges. Their desires were so strong they couldn't disengage from each other's arms long enough to continue their lovemaking on their bed.

Clothing was ripped from their bodies as they consummated their lust for each other. Only after that first joining could they control themselves long enough to make it into the bedroom and continue their lovemaking.

They eventually woke in each other's arms. Alice said, "What was that about? That was even stronger than the time you first mind touched with me."

"That's a first for me. Are we both going through another change? Did I hurt you? My attraction for you was so strong I couldn't control myself. I couldn't even think. My carnal urges were so strong all I could do was make love to you."

Alice examined herself and found several tender places, but no cuts or bleeding. She tenderly examined Aaron's limp male appendage, but it seemed none the worse because of their activity. "It's a good thing we weren't wearing our silks or we might've hurt ourselves trying to get them off."

They left the bed and stood under the full body shower set at the hottest water temperature they could stand. Standing under the shower in Aaron's arms she mentally opened herself to his probe. He soon withdrew and told her to probe his mind.

Alice withdrew from his mind and looked at Aaron in confusion. "What does this mean?"

"I don't know other than we are more powerful than we were before."

"Aaron, I feel strong again; not like I felt before our sex workout. It's like I'm primed for action of some kind."

"Let's get dressed and experiment. Maybe we can determine if anything's changed."

Later, they sat down together on the couch and Aaron said, "Let's open our minds and search for anything involving the Guild."

They immediately got the same hit and began following the thoughts of someone talking on a com. After listening to the one-sided conversation for a short period of time, Alice was able to find and follow both sides of the conversation. The two parties were talking about taking their mother into the Temple for an appointment with the Blues for a medical treatment.

Aaron and Alice left this conversation and began another search. They soon had different hits and each followed their own finds. Aaron's was another innocent occurrence, but Alice's showed promise and he joined her thoughts.

The person's mental thoughts they were following was thinking about stealing the gold stored in the San Francisco Temple. The stories he or she heard was that all the west coast's Guild revenue had been accumulating for decades and was stored there. They had a group of ten people who were going to enter through the front door of the Temple at midnight and force someone to take them to the storage room.

Alice said, "He or she is clueless about how finances are handled within the Guild. These people are going to hurt someone if they follow through with their plan. Obviously, they must be from the Bay area and my reading places them in that direction."

"I think you're right. I've been there before and stayed at a local hotel. Let's pack a bag for three days and get into our silks before we leave."

After arriving at the hotel they left their luggage in their room while they followed the mental thoughts of the person with criminal intent to his or her location. The robo cab let them out a block past the house they were now watching and mentally listening to the occupants' conversations.

They could tell there were at least three people inside making plans to rob the temple tomorrow night. Aaron said, "Let's try to get a visual reading of the subjects' faces and the house's layout in case we want to teleport inside later."

Satisfied they had all the information they needed, they teleported to the San Francisco Temple. They walked up to the reception desk, and since they were in street clothing Aaron asked that a security representative meet them. Soon a large Blue male approached them and said, "I'm Security Agent Josh Madison. Do you have a problem?"

They both showed their ID's and asked to speak to the person in charge. Agent Madison escorted them to the security office area and knocked on a door labeled Director. Upon hearing "Enter" Madison led Aaron and Alice into the room where a petite redheaded woman sat behind a desk that almost dwarfed her. Her sharp eyes and strong voice soon dispelled the notion that she was not fit for her position.

"Josh, what's the problem?"

Alice stepped forward and showing her ID. "Director, we are Special Agents for the Priestess and bring unwelcome news."

"Crap! You must be the team who took care of the Baltimore mess. I'm Director Abigail Carson and you're Alice Jackson, so the big guy must be Aaron Pearson. What's headed our way?"

Aaron said, "A team of about ten people who think you have a fortune in gold stored in the Temple. They plan on coming in tomorrow night and our best chance of getting all of them is when they enter the lobby."

"What! We don't store gold here. Are they some kind of nuts?"

Alice smiled at her response. "Obviously, they are not very bright, but they still present a threat to the Temple and its people. We propose to lay a trap for them which will be sprung when they enter the lobby area."

Director Carson intently looked at the pair before coming to a decision. "Eyewitnesses at the Baltimore flap report that you both have strong teleportation and mind control powers. In fact my security sensors report that you arrived here by teleportation."

The Director suddenly shook her head. "I don't know why I'm hesitating. You have the authority to order me to do anything you want. Obviously you feel confident in your abilities."

Alice gave her a small smile before saying, "Director Carson we are the strongest members of the Guild, made even stronger by being mated. We are still learning the extent of our powers, so yes we feel confident in our ability to handle this group. We need at least three of your security personnel outside to handle those would-be thieves who were left with their transportation. I assume they will have stolen heavy trucks to handle the gold they plan on taking. Now let's go over what we plan on doing to catch these people."

The following evening at nine p.m., the Temple's unlocked doors burst open with a horde of masked men entering the lobby. They pointed weapons at the two people manning the reception booth and demanded to know where the gold was stored. The whole masked group suddenly dropped to the floor as if someone had flipped a switch. Aaron and Alice left the booth where they were joined by the Temple's security staff, which began putting restraints on the intruders.

Director Carson joined Aaron and Alice. "My people captured four more outside and the police are on the way. It looks like your plan worked perfectly, no fuss, no bother. How many do you have here?"

Aaron replied, "Eight! Apparently they recruited more people since we last touched the minds of the leaders. When the police arrive we'll wake them so that they will be easier to move."

Alice said, "In your report to the Priestess please add any comments you like on how better we can serve the Guild. Our own report will reflect your willingness to work with us to resolve this problem."

Director Carson gave them a satisfied smile and shook their hands. "Feel free to stop by if you are passing through, but I hope we can return to our uneventful status now. Do you have any recommendations for our staff?"

Aaron laughed as he had a thought. "You should consider dispelling the rumor about gold being stored here. Maybe have guided tours of the Temple explaining how everything works."

"Point taken. I'll include that in my report to the Priestess."

Aaron and Alice took their leave after awakening the thieves when the police arrived, and then teleported back to their hotel room. They quickly shed their clothing and took a shared shower that soon became a carnal experience as they made love. Alice pulled her mate out of the shower and after toweling each other dry, they continued their lovemaking on the bed. Room service interrupted their basking glow of fulfillment. Aaron quickly donned a robe and brought their order into the room. Then shedding the robe he returned to the bed and hand fed his mate morsels of food, which she reciprocated.

CHAPTER EIGHT

Early the next morning they teleported to the door of their supervisor's office, Natalie Bertram. Entering, Aaron asked to see the Director.

Looking up at her two agents, Natalie said, "I've received Director Carson's report of your actions last night. Basically she says you two can walk on water. What's the real story?"

Alice quipped, "We walk on water. Seriously, we followed a lead to San Francisco were we found a plot to steal the Temple's gold supply. We enlisted the help of the Temple's security personnel and captured all the people involved in the plot without any injuries. When we left the Temple the police were carting them out of the premises."

"Gold supply! We don't store gold. Where did they get the idea we had any gold?"

Aaron replied, "Speculation that morphs into a rumor, that then becomes common knowledge. We recommended that the Temple include how it transfers funds in its future tours."

Director Bertram frowned at him. "It's not going to help our cause when the public hears about the attempt to steal our gold and how strong our security was to catch them."

Alice frowned, "Stupid greedy people may still think there's gold there, but the smart greedy ones will know better. The smart ones are more dangerous."

"Regardless, you two have performed well. Even better than I expected and the Priestess is very pleased. How are you feeling, any backlash from use of your powers?"

Aaron and Alice looked at each other as they mentally conferred, then Aaron replied, "We found that if we do repeated teleportation's in a short period of time it drains our energy reserves to the point of exhaustion. Food and rest seemed to cure this problem though. We did have another extreme sexual attack similar to when Alice gained my powers. We mentally checked each other and found increased capacity for both of us. However, we haven't yet determined any increased performance in our powers."

Director Bertram looked at her two agents with concern. "Let me know if you have any problems. In the meantime take a rest somewhere quiet, like a beach. Sit under an umbrella and have one of those drinks with rum and fruit in it."

Pulling a brochure out of a drawer she slid it across to Alice. "Whoa, this looks beautiful and it even has a picture of the hotel. Aaron, let's do it."

Director Bertram winked at Aaron, who then smiled before saying, "Honey I don't think the world is ready to see you on the beach. I'm afraid when people see your exposed body and their resulting lustful thoughts occur, I'd attack them in a fit of jealousy."

"Oh baby. I'm taking the same risk with you," Alice said with a wicked smile as she ran a finger down his cheek.

"Get out of here you two oversexed beasts!"

After they teleported out of the room, Natalie smiled in satisfaction. *I hope they have fun. This is the only way I could think of to ensure they recharge their energy.*

After packing their bags they teleported to the hotel in the brochure and were immediately struck by the high humidity, causing them to realize they were overdressed. After checking in and following a bellboy to their room, their eyes were drawn to the nearby beach where waves were gently breaking. Fifteen minutes later they were wetting their toes in the Caribbean waters.

Alice was curious as to the beach attire others were wearing, but soon discovered less clothing and more skin was the norm here. She thought, *Wow! Over half the women aren't wearing tops and the bottoms leave nothing to the imagination, especially the men's.*

Aaron mentally replied, *you look sexier covered than most of those naked women.*

Oh, that's just your Midwestern moral upbringing, although some of those women should cover up that flab.

Aaron put his arm around her waist and they walked to the nearest beach bar for an umbrella rum fruit drink. Sitting under an awning out of the sun they sipped their drinks and watched the people walk by and enjoyed the breeze off the ocean. He kissed his mate and said, "I'm going after some sun screen and be right back."

Alice ordered another drink for them and was starting to relax while closing her eyes, when someone's X-rated thoughts intruded into her solitude. She raised her eyelids enough to scan those around her until she found the lecherous pig whose thoughts were beginning to make her mad. He was holding an almost full iced drink, which she caused to spill onto his lap.

With a startled oath he scrambled to his feet and then looked around to see if anyone noticed. Looking disgruntled he walked to the ocean and cleaned himself off. Aaron sat down next to her and said, "Good work. I was about to take a more direct approach."

"I got you another drink, so cool off. I've had plenty of practice with these kind of people."

"Yes dear. Hey this is good, what is it?"

"I don't know. I just pointed to a drink someone else had. It's a little sweet for me, but I still like it."

Putting their drinks down they quickly sprayed the sunscreen onto their exposed skin. "I'm glad you got this sun protection because I was starting to burn."

After they were at the beach for three days they decided to try somewhere different and teleported to the mountains above Denver. Upon arrival, Alice breathed in the cool crisp air in relief and smiled at Aaron. "Oh, this is so much better!"

"Yeah, let's check in and see what this place offers."

* * *

After three days they were so bored they returned to their apartment and resumed trolling for trouble. They decided to try merging their minds in their search efforts rather than trolling separately and discovered a whole new world opening to them. It was almost like opening a book titled thoughts about the Healing Guild, then turning to the section labeled adverse conspiracy.

This section was large as they considered where to start. Alice mentally touched the first listing and received a sour taste. She then sampled the next listing and got a repeat of the sour taste, only slightly stronger. They conferred and decided to skip to the last entry. Aaron's touch gave them a rotten taste so powerful they both gagged, but with forced resolve they followed the entry to its source.

They were surprised and sickened by what they discovered. There was a conspiracy within the Dallas Temple to replace its Priestess with the First Director, Victoria Mays. Included in her backers was the majority of the security detail, including its head, Katie Lee Draper. The only good thing was they were not yet ready to put their plan in action.

Aaron mentally contacted Natalie to expect their arrival soon with code red information. Aaron and Alice withdrew from their mind merge and physically held each other tightly, drawing strength from each other before teleporting to Natalie's office where she waited calmly for their report while they centered ourselves. They looked at each other for a moment before Alice said, "You do it!"

"We have new powers that while experimenting we discovered a conspiracy against the Dallas Priestess!" He then relayed what we had discovered.

While Aaron was telling his story Natalie's face became white with shock soon followed by her whole body stiffening as she slowly rose from behind her desk, her face flushed with anger. She seemed to glare at the two messengers as if it were their fault for bringing her this news, but as she regained her composure and her temper she slowly sat back down and considered her options.

"Did you discover when this coup was supposed to happen?"

Alice answered, "No, but we got the impression that it was

going to happen soon. Director Bertram, we can return and eliminate the problem before it happens, but what then? The structure of the Dallas Temple is rotten and drastic cuts are going to be needed."

She looked at Alice as if just now realizing what a sharp tool she had at her disposal. She gave the two standing before her a look of amazement and then slowly nodded her head. "Follow me! We are going to speak to the High Priestess."

The High Priestess looked up from her desk as they entered her domain. " Natalie, what's going on? This must be very important."

"Priestess, I'm sorry for this interruption but our agents have uncovered a conspiracy to unseat the Dallas Priestess by its First Director."

She turned to Aaron. "Repeat what you told me."

After Aaron had finished his tale the High Priestess looked at him in shock and dismay, then she turned to Natalie. "This is terrible! What do you recommend?"

"Priestess, have you had any recent contact with the Dallas Priestess and if so, did she appear well?"

"I talked to her last week and she appeared well then. We talked for about twenty minutes about the condition of the Dallas Region and I'm sure she was not mentally incapacitated. It must be the First Director who is at fault."

"Yes, you are most likely correct in your judgment. I'm not aware of this happening in the past before, how about you?"

The High Priestess looked at us for a moment before answering. "It has happened once before about eighty years ago in Dallas. Is it possible that the First Director there is related to anyone involved in that attack?"

"Possibly, how was the first instance resolved?"

"The Dallas security detail stopped it after the Priestess was killed."

"The security detail is part of this conspiracy, so that won't happen this time. However, we have Aaron and Alice who say they can stop it, but that still leaves the question of what to do with all the others who are involved."

"I see your point. When we remove them there is going to be a big hole to fill. There is no way to keep this attempted coup a secret. Perhaps our members should be aware of our past problems so that they can guard against this happening again. They should also be aware that we have guardians to protect ourselves against this threat in the future."

Natalie nodded her head in agreement. "Very well. These guardians have gotten even more powerful since you last met them. With your permission I plan on sending security from several other Temples to assist them in this response."

"Very well, but please remove the Dallas Priestess from harm's way before proceeding. Bring her here for safekeeping."

The Priestess bid us a 'Go with God' farewell as we left her office. After we returned to Natalie's office she asked, "How many people do you need?"

Alice asked, "How big is Dallas' security force?"

"About half what we have here, say fifteen, no more than twenty."

Aaron thought a moment. "We can freeze any we meet, but the Temple will need security when we replace the old force - so we better take twenty. Later we can replace these with permanent staff. Alice and I can teleport personnel faster than they can get there otherwise. Show us pictures of the Temple locations where they will be picked up and somewhere near the Dallas Temple where we can meet."

Forty minutes later Aaron and Alice with twenty experienced security personnel were less than a block from the Dallas Temple. Included in each five person team was that Temple's second in command, and they were all more than ready to right the disloyalty of Dallas' security force. Aaron told the others, "Alice and I are going in to bring out the Priestess before we begin the assault, so stay out of sight until I return. Alice is taking the Priestess to Kansas City, then will return to join us in this fight."

The four team leaders gave us a salute before we teleported to the Priestess's chamber. We looked around the empty room, but quickly followed the sound of voices where five men were trying to bind the Priestess's hands. We froze the men in place and freed the Priestess while informing her of our identity and our plans. Alice then teleported the Priestess and herself to the High Priestess's office before returning to Dallas to join Aaron and the assault force.

When Alice materialized beside Aaron they all walked to the Temple with the two guardians leading the way. Aaron and Alice started freezing the local security personnel in place as they worked their way toward the First Director's office. Their own force placed restraints on the local security people already incapacitated as they advanced.

Aaron and Alice entered the First Director's office where they found Director Victoria Mays and Security Head Katie Lee Draper. They turned in surprise as we entered the room, with Draper quickly reaching for her weapon. Alice froze her arm, leaving her able to talk.

Aaron smiled at the two. "Surprise! Your plot is over. Now tell me what you expected to achieve from your actions?"

Director Mays threw a paperweight at him, which Aaron easily caught one handed before returning it to her desk. "That wasn't nice. Why don't you two sit down on the couch over there and tell us all about your plans. If you don't we'll freeze the both of you and set you in a dark room until you're ready to talk. What's it going to be?"

Mays glared at the two guardians for a moment then asked, "What about my people?"

Alice smiled and answered, "They were no problem and have been restrained until we can sort them out."

Draper grimaced. "The ones who refused to go along with us are all locked up in our holding cells."

Alice thought to Aaron, *that makes it easier. I'll pass that information to our people.*

Aaron removed Draper's weapon and helped her sit on the couch, then pointed where Mays was to join her. "Okay, you should have realized by now that you have no chance of realizing your goal, so tell me what you hoped to gain. If you don't we can pull it from your minds with little effort on our part, but not without some discomfort to you. It's your choice."

Mays glared at Aaron with such hate that if he'd been made of ice he would have melted. Alice mentally pictured throwing icy water on them and both reacted as if it actually occurred, with Mays and Draper gasping for air and screaming in fright.

Alice mentally screamed at them, *tell us why you did this*

despicable thing!

They cringed with eyes wide in fear as they looked at Alice whose white aura was pulsating in time with her heartbeat. Draper blurted, "She did it because of what happened when her family tried to revolt before!"

"Why did you support her in this unholy plan?"

"I was promised the First Director's position once she was made Priestess."

"You're as crazy as Mays if you believed this revolt could succeed. The High Priestess would have leveled this Temple to the ground before letting you prevail."

Draper's face suddenly turned white as she realized the truth in the statement. "I throw myself at the High Priestess's mercy. I was blinded by greed and the promises of Director Mays!"

Alice mentally asked Aaron, *Do we need anything more?*

No. But next time I want to be the bad guy.

Alice contacted Control and gave her a status report, followed by a request for any instructions. Director Bertram's reply was incredulous; *you mean that this was sour grapes for not getting their way in the last revolt! The High Priestess will pass judgment on these two after they are brought to Kansas City. The others in the revolt will receive a partial mind wipe and reassignment. After you bring the two here you can return the Priestess to Dallas and help getting her Temple in order.*

CHAPTER NINE

Aaron and Alice had been in Dallas a week helping the Priestess fill the holes left in her security staff before they were comfortable leaving. The vacant Directorship was something left for someone of higher rank to take care of.

They returned to Kansas City to report their task completed. Director Bertram gazed at her two agents with satisfaction and complimented them on a job well done. "Before you two start something else take a few days off and recharge. I have no pressing need for your talents, so enjoy yourselves."

Aaron and Alice returned to their apartment and did some housekeeping chores until bedtime where they discussed what to do on their time off. Alice snuggled against her mate inhaling his distinctive scent until she used her tongue to taste her lover. "Honey, we could visit your parents for a few days. I'm sure they would be happy to see us and your Mom is probably dying to hear what happened at the Dallas Temple."

Aaron chuckled. "Yeah, I want to go home too. We both need to decompress for a few days before opening more of those files we found. Your mother is probably sick of seeing us after all the time we spent with her in Dallas, besides the Temple there still leaves a bad taste in my mouth."

Aaron mentally informed his parents of their plans and they

fell asleep in each other's arms. Joan wanted them to come for breakfast, so they set their wake up alarm early because of the time difference in Baltimore.

Aaron and Alice arrived in his parent's living room, dropped their bags and yelled that they had arrived. Joan laughed, "I thought that noise was you two. Come in here and sit down, breakfast is ready."

When they entered the kitchen Joan and Robert greeted their son and Alice with kisses and hugs. After they were seated Joan looked at us with concern. "You both are now even more powerful! You actually have a glow about you. What has happened?"

Alice took Joan's hand and squeezed it slightly. "We had another surge which has given us additional powers that we haven't fully explored yet. So far it has been very helpful in performing our job."

Aaron gave a short chuckle before quickly covering his mouth with his hand. His mother looked at him sharply. "What are you not telling me?"

Aaron embarrassingly looked at Alice and shook his head in disgust with himself. Alice stuck her tongue out at him. *You let it slip so you try to explain it!*

"Mom, Alice and I are the strongest Guild members in the world. We become even stronger when we are in mind meld. In addition, we were recently given additional powers that we are still exploring."

Robert shook his head and slowly smiled. "Apparently, you two don't know how strong you are."

Alice gave him a small smile. "Not really."

* * *

A week later they were back in their apartment in Kansas City. They both had a good time visiting Aaron's parents. His parents wanted to hear the inside scoop about the scandal in the Dallas Temple and were very impressed with the part their son and his mate played in stopping the revolt.

Aaron asked Alice, "Are you ready to open another of the stinky files?"

"I guess so. It's been over an hour since I've eaten so I should be able to keep it down."

They merged their minds and opened the file selecting the worst tasting item. After they read the contents they looked glumly at each other. Alice shook her head in disgust. "Well, this is crap. It's not as bad as the first one, but people are really dumb!"

Aaron nodded his head in agreement. "I'll notify Control that we need to conference. What say, fifteen minutes?"

"Okay, I need to take a bathroom break before we go."

They arrived at the appointed time in Director Bertram's office. She pointed to her chairs when they arrived and waited until they were seated before asking, "What's wrong this time?"

Alice grimaced. "It's the Sidney, Australia Temple this time. The First Director refuses to accept qualified and tested Red and Blue applicants who have any aboriginal blood."

Bertram's face turned almost purple in anger. "That's specifically forbidden in the Temple's

Bylaws! How long has this been going on?"

Aaron said, "Since First Director Seth Adamson was appointed last year - about ten months."

"Why was this not reported by the Temple's Security Head?"

"We don't know. That will need to be investigated as well. This is another example of what happens when the First Director is not a Guild member."

"How soon can you get there and report?"

Alice responded, "Soon! Should we relieve the First Director of his duties until a replacement is available?"

"Yes, if he is violating the Temple's Bylaws. If the Security Head is derelict in his duties then he should be removed as well. Use your diplomat passports if they are still current."

Five hours later they were at the Sidney, Australia Temple asking the reception clerk to notify the Security Head they needed to see him. A security staff member soon escorted them to his office. Aaron and Alice displayed their pin and written authorization to Ralph Meeker, who looked at them in surprise.

"So you must be the new troubleshooters for the High Priestess. What can I do for you?"

Aaron said, "How long have you been in your position here?"

"About ten months, why?"

"What did you do before you became Head of Security here."

"I was second of security at the Auckland, New Zealand Temple."

"Were you aware that all the Temples have bylaws that prohibit discrimination of any kind?"

"Yes. What's the problem?"

"First Director Adamson has not accepted any qualified mixed-blood Red and Blue applicants."

"What! That can't be right. I check every rejected applicant's file and none were tagged as qualified."

"We have a list of qualified applicants that were rejected. Check them against your list."

Meeker quickly compared his list against theirs and said in confusion, "None of yours is on my list."

Alice asked, "Who provides you with the reject listing?" "The First Director personally brings it to me so no one can alter it. Crap-a-doddle! He altered it."

Aaron said, "We believe you. We have monitored your memories during this conversation and what you told us was the truth, as you know it. We want you and at least two other security personnel to physically remove the First Director from his office and put him under lockdown. We will then do a search for the missing files."

Two hours later they had physical evidence of Adamson's misconduct when they found the missing files. Aaron placed Meeker in temporary charge of the Temple until a replacement was found and gave him instructions to hire all those qualified applicants previously rejected.

They checked what the time difference was in Kansas City and decided to teleport to their apartment for a few hours of sleep before reporting to Control. It was three a.m. in Kansas City when they teleported to their apartment. They shared a shower before setting the wake-up for eight a.m. and snuggled together in bed.

CHAPTER TEN

The increasing volume of the wake-up brought them out of their deep sleep. Alice quickly got out of bed and hit the off switch, then gazed with love at her mate who was just rising from their bed.

"Not so fast Aaron, you have to do your mate duty you felt too tired to do last night." Whereupon he groaned and held open his arms as she crawled into his arms like a big cat after her prey. They kissed, then Alice slowly licked her way down his chest taking small bites until she got to his center. Aaron's reaction was swift as he held her head in place and groaned in appreciation.

She looked up at him with a smile of satisfaction. "Now you are ready," she said as she climbed astride him and they began their dance of love. Eventually their lust was sated and she slid off to lay beside him with a satisfied smile on her face.

Aaron playfully kissed her on the nose. "If you're ready we need to get to work."

She groaned, but gave him a lazy smile. "We can save time if we shower together."

"Okay, but no hanky-panky or we'll never get there."

She stuck her tongue out at him. "Spoil sport!"

Once finished with their shower and dressed, Alice called Control and made an appointment in twenty minutes. They prepared a breakfast meal for themselves, then checked each other's appearance before teleporting to Director Bertram's office.

Bertram looked up when they appeared before her desk. "How did it go?"

Aaron answered, "About what we expected. The First Director altered the files to hide what he'd been doing. Security Head Ralph Meeker had no idea what was going on. We had him lock up Adamson until you decide what to do with him and placed Meeker in temporary charge. We told Meeker to hire the rejected qualified Reds and Blues, so that problem should now be resolved."

Bertram's face slowly transformed into a smile as she gazed at her two agents. "This project of mine is working out quite well for us. Do you have any problems or questions?"

They looked at each other for a moment before Alice spoke, "We need to take some time to experiment with our new abilities. We feel that it's important before we continue with our assignments."

"How much time do you think you need?"

Aaron responded, "We don't know, but if it takes more than a week we'll check back with you."

Bertram thoughtfully looked at them for a few moments. "Okay, but if we have a crisis I'll contact you. Go on and do your thing."

The two teleported back to their apartment and sat at their kitchen table contemplating their next move. Alice asked, "Where should we start?"

He shrugged his shoulders. "Let's merge our minds and slowly expand our awareness. Maybe we can learn something that way."

They slowly reached out with their merged mind, first being aware of the minds of these people nearby, then as they reached further out they were subjected to the clamor of thousands of minds. Before expanding further they placed a selective block against all the mind chatter except those involving the Guild. This was much better and they were able to concentrate on anything new they encountered.

They continued their mind expansion until they slowly became aware of a pulse that grew stronger as their consciousness expanded. Eventually they stopped and studied this new phenomenon. It wasn't long before they realized the pulse matched the surge of blood through their body at each heartbeat.

They wondered if this was only feedback from their expanded awareness or something else entirely. Suddenly, they were standing together on a hilltop overlooking a beautiful meadow. Alice thought it was the most peaceful sight she had even seen when she was startled by a soft voice behind them.

"Yes, it has a calming effect doesn't it."

They quickly turned to find Barbara, the legendary Messenger Angel, standing before them with a slight smile on her face. "Surprise! If only you knew how you two bring back good memories of Angel and her trials as she found her way through God's plan. Your task is similar. As with Angel, you have been given gifts to aid you in your journey of discovery. I will reappear as you need me and eventually you will be aided by your children."

She disappeared, leaving them with open mouths and unasked questions on their tongues. Aaron hugged his mate tightly in a loving embrace. "Barbara said we will have children," he said softly.

"I know. But she didn't say when and what our task is supposed to be. The legend mentioned that Barbara often spoke in riddles, but always told the truth. We must remember to ask what our task is, otherwise we may chase our tails. Let's return to the Temple and ask to speak to the High Priestess."

Aaron nodded his head. "I'll inform Control that we are returning."

She looked again at the peaceful valley and breathed in the sweet scent of the meadow before they teleported. Director Bertram breathed in the sweet fragrance they brought with them and smiled in appreciation. "That was quick. What's going on?"

Alice smiled. "We had another visit from Barbara and we need to speak to the High Priestess."

Bertram's mouth opened in surprise, then in understanding. "Sit and I'll make it happen."

Ten minutes later they were all standing before the High Priestess. "Well, what's happened?"

Aaron explained their meeting with Barbara and her brief message to them. Alice continued, "Barbara compared us to Angel Pearson who she guided along God's path. Apparently, she is now going to do the same with Aaron and myself. Do we have access to the original or copy of Barbara's self-portrait?"

The High Priestess looked at her in surprise as she realized the reason for the request. "Yes! Follow me."

They soon entered a room whose only furnishing was Barbara's self-portrait. A spotlight on the painting was the room's only illumination. The High Priestess said, "Our ancestors sealed the painting in a special gas case to protect it from further deterioration, much like the Declaration of Independence. I come here quite often to seek love and peace. Can you feel the love emanating from the painting?"

Aaron nodded his head before saying, "I know all the women Guild members resemble Barbara, but look at Alice and the painting - they are the spitting image of each other."

They compared Barbara's image to Alice, then Aaron asked, "Do we have a picture of Angel?"

The High Priestess smiled at him. "Remember, I took that name when I became High Priestess. Follow me."

They soon entered a room that could only be her private quarters. Hanging on the wall much like Barbara's painting was a painting of a beautiful woman with white hair. "This painting was done by Elizabeth Pearson, Angel's younger sister. Besides being a healer she became a well-known painter. This painting was not generally known outside the family. Alice, stand beside the painting and let's see how you two compare."

Alice did as asked. "Besides the hair color how do I compare?"

Aaron took in a gasp of air. "Apparently, Angel's painting was done when she was about the same age as Alice. Add white hair to Alice and they are the same face."

The High Priestess nodded her head in agreement. "From my readings of Angel's personality, Alice has other similarities. Okay, what does this tell us besides they look alike and share personality traits?"

Aaron replied, "Barbara has a strong tie to Alice and said that we have a task to perform for God. I think Alice needs to ask Barbara for more details."

The High Priestess looked at Director Bertram questioningly, who then nodded her head. Bertram said, "Okay, Alice lead the way."

They all returned to Barbara's painting where Alice took a step before the others and spoke, "Barbara you were too cryptic in our previous meeting. Would you please explain what Aaron and I are expected to do?"

Barbara seemed to step out of her painting and stood before the group, causing a gasp of surprise and awe from the High Priestess and Director Bertram. "I expect you to continue as before and accumulate a history of accomplishments that elevate your reputation to where evildoers will think twice before attempting crimes against the Guild. In addition, word of my return will strengthen the Guild's resolve to serve God's will. I will return when you need me."

She returned to her painting and continued her projection of love. The High Priestess rose from the floor where she had knelt when Barbara first appeared. "I must make an announcement of Barbara's message. Director Bertram would you and our agents consult with me on what I should reveal?"

Bertram said, "Of course, let's retire to your office."

CHAPTER ELEVEN

Later that day Aaron and Alice were back in their apartment considering what they should do next. Alice suggested, "Let's pick an assignment that will make a big splash within the Guild."

"You mean one as big or greater than the Dallas revolt?"

"Yeah, like that," she said with a rueful smile.

"Okay, let's see what we have to choose from."

They merged their minds and opened the stinky file and pulled three of the worst smelling files for review and settled on one that met their needs. Alice shook her head; "We better put on our silks now as time is short on this one!"

"Okay, you start while I notify Control on what and where we're going."

They soon teleported to the London Temple where they informed the receptionist they were agents of the High Priestess and wished an immediate meeting with the Head of Security. Two security guards quickly escorted them to her office. As they entered, Lauren McCormick rose from her desk and greeted them with a grimace of concern. "Saints be praised, I hope you're not here with a problem about our Temple!"

Aaron shook his head, "No, but we need your help with a problem at the Glasgow Temple."

"Certainly, what kind of help do you need?"

"We have intelligence that the Temple is going to be attacked soon by a large group whose intention is to destroy the Temple and all who are in it. We think they plan to use a large bomb to achieve their goal."

"Okay, tell me what you need."

Aaron looked at Alice and at her nod said, "We need at least fifteen of your security staff to ring the perimeter of the Temple for three blocks. The Glasgow staff and we will protect the Temple. Have your staff use their telepathic ability to monitor anyone passing through their ring and let us know when they are coming. How soon can you have them ready so we can teleport them to the Temple?"

Twenty minutes later they had teleported the London security personnel to the Glasgow, Scotland Temple and were bringing its Security Head up to date. Mary Anne Peterson's face showed her anger at the news of an imminent attack against her Temple. "Why us? Everyone likes us here."

Alice replied, "It's not your specific Temple. They have a hatred for the Healing Guild as a whole. We think they picked you because of your small size and security staff. They are going to be surprised by what they find when they begin their attack. Reschedule all your appointments today so that we can avoid those people getting hurt."

Thirty-five minutes later they received their first report of attackers walking through their perimeter in small groups from at least four different streets. Aaron said, "Mary Anne, use your staff to prevent anyone from entering the Temple, while we will go outside and do the same."

Aaron and Alice levitated themselves above the Temple and placed a force barrier around the Temple. When the first attackers reached the invisible barrier they bounced back with many falling to the ground. Realizing that they couldn't get through the barrier they started looking around and spotted the two agents hanging in the air above the Temple. They started firing projectable weapons at the agents hoping to kill them, but their shots were all deflected by the force field.

Others in the attacking group soon arrived and joined in firing at the agents. Alice froze all of them in place, including two who were pushing a cart that was probably carrying their bomb. The security forces from the London Temple soon arrived and bound their captives for eventual handover to the local police.

Dropping the barrier Aaron and Alice joined the security force and checked the cart. Looking inside they discovered what appeared to be a explosive device that was attached to a timer counting down to zero with less than six minutes to detonation. Aaron and Alice conferred mentally until they quickly reached a consensus, then acted. The cart started raising slowly, then faster until it quickly disappeared through the late morning clouds. Less than five minutes later there was a glaring light, brighter than the sun. Later the faint sound of a grumbling explosion reached them, almost like thunder from a faraway storm.

Alice mentally asked Aaron, *was that a small nuke?*

He replied, "Let's check the two people who were with the cart to try to find the bomb maker."

They scanned the memories of the two bomb carriers that gave them a name and a mental picture of the person they sought. They mentally passed this information to all the local Guild members in hopes they had seen him, then to all worldwide Guild members explaining why they needed to find him and to contact the Kansas City Temple with any knowledge.

The security team made mental scans of their captives that resulted in information about their organization, safe house's, and membership. However, no knowledge was gained about the bomb or its maker.

Alice mentally called Control to notify her of their imminent arrival. They told the security personnel to maintain a watch over their captives, then teleported to Kansas City. Director Bertram had a concerned expression on her face when the two agents materialized in her office.

"What on earth happened in Glasgow? The newsies are awash with conflicting reports of a huge explosion about 500 miles above Scotland!"

Alice gave Aaron a concerned look. "Is that far enough to avoid any radiation fallback?"

"I think so. The Earth's natural protection from the Sun's radiation should work in our favor. Director Bertram we captured all the people who attempted to destroy the Glasgow Temple. No injuries were suffered and the Temple appeared to be unharmed."

He then explained their experience with the bomb and their

plans to find its maker. Bertram gazed at her two star agents with pride and awe. They had far exceeded anyone's expectation and if the situation demanded it, they without hesitation made decisions that would affect all mankind.

"Alright, I agree with your plan and I'll pass on any information that we obtain. You two have done well and this business will certainly get the attention Barbara alluded too. Let me know if there is anything you need. Get back there and attend to business!"

Aaron and Alice returned to the Glasgow Temple twenty minutes after leaving for Kansas City. Mary Ann Hicks, the London Head of Security, immediately came to them and gave an update of what transpired in their absence. The Glasgow Head of Security had called the local police who even now were starting to arrive.

Soon a police officer approached them. "I'm Lt. Jasper McPeters, who's in charge here?"

Aaron spoke, "Alice and I are. My name is Aaron Pearson and we represent the High Priestess of the Healing Guild's World Headquarters in Kansas City. These people in restraints were trying to destroy Glasgow's Temple with a bomb. We used our powers to throw it into space just before it exploded."

Lt. McPeters looked at the large group of people lying frozen on the street, and then said in a strangled voice, "Bomb! You two made it go into space? How can you do that?"

Lt. McPeters face had turned white by this time as he tried to reconcile what he was seeing with what he thought people could do. Mary Ann Hicks spoke, "I'm Head of Security at our London Temple and I saw them do it. We in the Guild all have special powers of varying degrees of strength. These two are reportedly the strongest in the Guild and they are mated, which makes them able to combine their powers."

Alice gave Lt. McPeters a small smile as she asked, "May I see your hand comp?"

In a daze he handed her his unit. She pressed buttons until getting the screen she wanted then mentally downloaded the name and picture of the bomber. Returning his comp she said, "Based upon our mental scans of the two bomb carriers this is the bomb maker. Maybe between the police and our efforts we can apprehend him before he makes another bomb."

Aaron asked, "If you are ready to take these people off our hands we will release them from their freeze status?"

Lt. McPeters nodded his head and the agents released the prisoners. Alice and Aaron then started teleporting the London security personnel back to their Temple. When all were back in London Aaron and Alice said their farewells and returned to their Kansas City apartment.

Finally alone they embraced and merged their minds seeking solace from the horrific calamity they had narrowly prevented. Finally centered they drew apart and Aaron said, "Let's eat something and regain our strength before we search for the bomber."

Alice nodded her head and hugged her mate before searching their cooler for something to eat. "Do you want protein or something sweet?"

"Do we have any honey buns left?"

"I should have known what your answer would be, let's see... Yep, there's two left. Just enough for me!"

She dodged his reaching hands while taking a bite out of a bun. "Oooh, that's goood!"

She tossed a bun to Aaron before he could retaliate. He took a bite and slowly chewed savoring its sweet taste. "Yeah, this is good. Let's be sure to get more of this brand."

"Yes dear. While this sugar is working I'm going to take a shower."

"Go ahead, I'll be right behind you as soon as I finish this last piece."

Forty minutes later they were back in the kitchen after their joint shower followed by a hot love session that began in the shower. Alice looked at her mate with a satisfied smile. "I hope you didn't use all your energy up because we need to find this guy."

"Yeah and I don't think Doran Gray, the name he was using, is going to be any help. Let's merge our minds and search for his thoughts."

They started their search in England and when that was fruitless, slowly moved east to Europe where after another hour of searching they got a hit. They soon narrowed their search to

France, then Paris where they were listening to someone thinking of getting material for another nuke. After another half hour they couldn't glean additional personal information so they disengaged their minds and using the Eiffel Tower as their destination they teleported.

They walked to a nearby kiosk that featured a map of Paris. Aaron pointed to the Arch of Triumph. "I'll teleport there and we'll try to get a triangulation on where he's at."

After his arrival he soon mentally reported, *from here he's east by southeast. Do the calculation and use the map to give us the nearest intersection.*

Alice drew a line with her finger from her position on the map, along the angle she deduced, to where it intersected with Aaron's line. *It looks like Avenue de Choisy and Rue de Tolbiac. Come back here and we'll take a robo cab.*

The cab brought them to their destination where the signal they had been following was now a few blocks South. It wasn't long before the cab stopped before a six-story apartment building. Alice nodded her head in satisfaction. "He's in the basement toward the rear of the building."

Aaron said, "Wait until I get into position behind the building, then we'll go in together."

About ten minutes later Alice mentally heard, *Okay, let's get this guy.*

The basement door was locked, but Alice easily tore it off the doorway with her powers. As she entered a long hallway she heard a loud bang from further ahead, which was Aaron's entrance. Two doors down a man stuck his head out and looked her way, then immediately ran away from her. He only took three steps before Alice froze him in place.

Aaron soon joined her and confirmed that this was indeed the bomber they sought. "Let's teleport him to Control."

"Wait! I'll let her know we're coming."

Director Bertram looked unsurprised when Aaron and Alice appeared with a frozen man. "Is this him? He certainly looks like the picture you posted."

Alice replied, "We thought you might want to be present when we interrogate him. Right now he's mentally screaming in fright."

"Yes, even I can hear his pleading. Wait a moment while I

contact the High Priestess."

Director Bertram's face showed her displeasure, then addressed her agents, "The High Priestess is otherwise indisposed, but will meet us in the conference room in fifteen minutes. She wants to meet this potential mass murderer and try to understand his motives."

Alice blurted, "Doesn't she realize that his mind is cracked?"

Director Bertram shrugged her shoulders. "She suspects as much, but still wants to personally examine him."

"Would you watch him while Aaron and I take a short bathroom break?"

"Fine. Use mine over there."

Fifteen minutes later they were waiting in the conference room with three additional security personnel including Head of Security Richard Simmons. He was questioning Aaron and Alice about how they had traced and brought the bomber here when the High Priestess entered the room.

She stood a moment gazing at the room's occupants before taking her chair. "Director Bertram how are you going to conduct the suspect's interrogation?"

"We are all telepaths, but not nearly as strong as our two agents. They will conduct the interrogation while we mentally observe. You may ask him questions after they finish. Is this satisfactory?"

"Yes, you may begin."

Aaron and Alice merged their minds and then slowly eased their way into his memories. His birth name is Randolph George Grant from London, England and graduated from a second tier University with help from a scholarship. His Physicist degree earned him a position in their R&D department with an arms manufacturing company. Ten years later he resigned after failing to receive what he considered a fair reward for his work in nuclear weapons. His girlfriend, Jill Gregory, was active in a fringe group who wanted a separate government for Ireland. Apparently, her small group was the only people interested in their goals. She convinced George, as she hated his first name Randolph, to use his talents to help their cause. Jill was one of the group captured in Glasgow.

Aaron and Alice withdrew from Randolph's mind and looked

at the High Priestess for any additional questions. She had a pained expression as she gazed at their prisoner, "That's all the motivation he had to murder thousands of people? He didn't even believe in her cause. Somehow he grew up without any teaching about what other people consider right and wrong."

Alice said, "Oh, he knew it was wrong. He just didn't care. Apparently he has no fear of God's wrath."

The High Priestess's face was red in anger. "Well, he's gotten a glimmer of what's coming his way now. It was God's will that gave you the powers to find and bring him before us. He will be brought before the World Court to answer for his crime. It will be either a mind wipe or death if found guilty. He will be given his choice."

Later, after the prisoner was turned over to the local police, Aaron and Alice were in Director Bertram's office receiving information on their duties when they would be called to testify at Grant's trial. The World Court is historically held at The Hague, Netherlands. Usually, from arrest to trial takes less than thirty days with most of that time seating three judges. No jury is called when proof of guilt testimony is psychic mind reading with two or more witnesses.

Director Bertram asked, "What now? You have achieved your goal of making yourselves known worldwide as its strongest psychics, who are agents of the Healing Guild. Agents whose goal is to search for evil within and outside the Guild that work against its activities to serve God's will."

Alice said, "Really? Worldwide? Maybe after the trial with its publicity."

Director Bertram pressed a button on her desk and a screen started streaming the world news-feed which showed their faces and names and then commentary of how they had saved Glasgow from a nuclear explosion, captured the attack force, and then tracked down the bomb maker hiding in Paris.

Aaron gave a snort of laughter. "Take that Alice. That will teach you not to make statements without full knowledge."

"Well, we have been a little busy. To answer your question, we'll continue with the next bad one on our list. But first Aaron and I are going to take a short break and visit our families as I suspect they are worried about us with all this publicity."

Director Bertram gave her a small smile. "Okay, but you two need to stay in the news to make this work. Go! Get out of here. I've got my own work to do."

After the two agents teleported she silently shook her head in amazement thinking, *those two are going to make history and not just by what they're doing now.*

CHAPTER TWELVE

Aaron and Alice agreed to visit Alice's parents first and after first letting her mother know they were arriving soon, they teleported to her living room. Rachel spoke from her kitchen, "I'm in here making lemonade, come and sit down with me."

They sat at the table while Rachel finished with the drink preparation and filled their glasses. Alice took a sip savoring her mother's recipe of the tart drink. "Ah, I've missed this."

Aaron took a large swallow, and then licked his lips in appreciation. "This is really good. What makes it different?"

Alice smiled, "It has two oranges that gives it a sweeter taste with less sugar. Well Mom, what do you think of your daughter's exploits?"

Rachel looked at her daughter uncertainly before glancing at Aaron who had a slight smile and a wicked gleam in his eyes. "Well honey, I don't think you did it all by yourself but I'm happy you and Aaron saved Glasgow from a horrible fate. Are you okay? You look a little stressed."

Aaron suddenly laughed at Alice's expression, who then threw a cookie at him. "I'm sorry Mom, I wasn't sure what to expect from you after all the news publicity we've gotten."

Rachel chuckled, then got up and pulled her daughter into a hug. "Alice, to me you will always be my little girl. But I see now that you have grown since you mated with Aaron. You both have changed. When you two arrived I could feel a strong presence and you both now have a faint glow. It must be your auras that I see. I've read the history of Angel and she glowed, especially when she used her powers. I think you both are even more powerful than she was."

Alice looked at her mother doubtfully. "More powerful than our founder? Is that possible?"

Aaron interrupted. "Alice, you bear the name of her daughter who was born stronger than Angel. Angel then acquired Alice's powers when they mind merged, much like we did."

Alice grimaced before replying, "Aaron, you were also given a name of the son of Alice, the first son of our legacy. That may be why you were given your special talent that I now share."

Rachel looked at them in shock. "You believe God has sent you on a task. That's why you are making the news, using your God given powers for the good of humanity."

Alice went to her mother and hugged her tightly, then led her to the couch where they sat facing each other while still holding hands. "Mom, we have had another visit from the angel Barbara. God wants us to remind everyone that he is still watching over everyone and is using Aaron and me as his tool. Don't be surprised when we are mentioned on the news again. Maybe you should call Joan, Aaron's mother, for mutual support if it becomes too stressful."

"Oh Alice, that is so like you. I've already done that. You two are a joy and sometimes a heartache for a mother when we fear for your safety. You won't fully understand that until you have your own children."

Alice shuddered at the thought. "I'm not ready for that. Can you imagine me raising kids?"

Rachel smiled at her daughter. "Remember, God has his plans for you. You will have children when He deems it appropriate."

* * *

Five days later they were back in their apartment returning from visiting Aaron's parents. His parents gave him the same support they found with Alice's family. It was late when they arrived and they were both tired from their interactions with family, so they opted for sleep as the proper remedy.

Alice was awakened by Aaron nibbling on her ear lobe, which immediately got her sexual engine running in high gear. She immediately flipped him over onto his back and lay on his chest looking into his surprised eyes. "Honey, you need to wake me like this more often. I think I'll give you a reward." She began passionately kissing him on the mouth then slowly kissing him down his body until she reached her goal, producing a strangled cry of passion from her mate. He suddenly reversed their positions and they made passionate love until they sated their passions.

They were lying in each other's arms almost too exhausted to move when Alice whispered, "We need to eat something to get our energy up before we can even take a shower. One of us needs to bring the other something. Baby, can you do it for me?"

Aaron chuckled. "I can try, but you now owe me if this happens again."

She kissed him in acceptance then moved aside as he weakly crawled off the bed and made his way into the kitchen. After several minutes Alice began to worry when she couldn't hear her mate's movements. She had about made up her mind to check on him when he returned bearing food.

"Ah, here you are. What have you brought me?" Alice worked herself up into a sitting position.

He gave her a tray containing a small box before getting into bed beside her. "I've never had this before so I picked it up the last time we shopped."

"What is it? Do I just open it up?"

"It's supposed to be an egg and biscuit sandwich. Touch the button on top and it warms it up."

They both initiated the warm-up procedure and waited, looking at their boxes for something to happen. Alice said, "Now what?"

Getting a blank expression from her mate she picked up her box and read the instructions. "It says to wait thirty seconds and open it. It's been that long already so I'll try mine."

She cautiously opened her box and was rewarded with an appetizing smell. She gingerly took the hot sandwich out of its container and bit into it, cautiously chewing slowly while murmuring in appreciation. Aaron followed her example and was soon eating his meal as well. Finishing their meal they took turns in the shower, not wanting to take a chance on wasting their energy on another sexual session. Recently they became aware that anytime they were naked together they had an almost overpowering desire to mate.

Aaron asked, "Are you ready for another task?"

"Alright, but we need to build up our reserves before we teleport again."

Aaron selected the next stinky file, which they examined together as a merged mind, then broke apart for discussion. "Aaron, it's good that we both have eidetic memories, otherwise we would have to stay merged to plan our strategy. This situation appears to be simple. Our temple in Peking, China is under threat of closure by the local Magistrate unless a bribe is paid to him. We can take direct action or report his criminal activity to the central government. I believe we need input from the High Priestess on this, do you agree?"

"Yes, I'll ask Control for an appointment."

After giving Control the details of their problem she told them to wait until she spoke with the High Priestess. They were eating a meal when Control told them to report to her office in thirty minutes.

Alice said, "That was quicker than expected. Is that good or bad?"

Aaron shrugged his shoulders. "Who knows? We better get there a little early so we can change into our Blues."

They soon teleported to the change room next to Director Bertram's office and when ready they knocked on the connecting door before entering her office. Director Bertram's face was grim as she motioned for them to follow her as they headed toward the High Priestess's office. The Priestess was praying at the small alter in her office, so they all bowed their heads in respect while they waited for her to finish. She soon finished her prayers and turned toward them.

"I was hoping for direct guidance, but as often is the case I must use my best judgment. The central government in Beijing can't be bothered by a case of bribery and told me to handle it. Before you teleport to China be sure you're wearing armor. If possible try not to be lethal. I would prefer the Temple be allowed to function. To assist you, here is a picture of the Peking Temple. May God be with you in your task."

They returned to Director Bertram's office where she gave them background information on the Peking Temple including the names of its Director and Head of Security. Since neither of the agents could speak the local language they were happy to learn their contacts spoke English. Alice asked, "What's the time difference there?"

Director Bertram said, "Thirteen hours ahead of us, so time your travel according to what you plan to do. Whatever actions you take make sure there is no blowback against the Temple. Take care and report when you are finished."

After changing, Aaron and Alice teleported back to their apartment and started to make plans. Thirty minutes later they knew what they had to do and made preparations to leave, including plans to wear their personal armor.

.

CHAPTER THIRTEEN

After taking a short nap they teleported to the front door of the Peking Temple and sought the Head of Security. Kimin Zhou didn't seem surprised at their arrival and spoke English with a British accent. "Your faces are on the streaming news and are quite famous, even here. I assume you are here to handle our problem with the local Magistrate."

Alice smiled. "It's good that you are aware of our efforts. I assume the Magistrate is also knowledgeable of our abilities?"

Zhou suddenly smiled. "That you are supermen and can fly and jump over tall buildings. Yes, if you confront him he will probably shit himself."

Aaron frowned, "Or immediately try to kill us! What time is it here?"

"Six p.m., it is our traditional evening dinner time."

Aaron looked at Alice and smiled before asking, "Zhou, have you been in his dwelling?"

"Yes, when he called the Director and myself to demand a bribe."

"May we scan your memory of that event so we can teleport into the dwelling?"

Zhou looked at them in surprise, then understanding, before saying, "Yes!"

The agents merged minds and scanned his mind until they got the visuals they needed. Withdrawing, they smiled and thanked him before vanishing with a small popping sound as air filled the void when they teleported. They reappeared in the Magistrate's dining area and immediately froze everyone in the room.

After doing a scan they determined the only other people in the building were guards at the exits. Alice pointed at the only male in the room dressed in finery. "That's the Magistrate!"

They planted a false memory in the Magistrate's brain that gave him a warm fuzzy feeling when he thought about the Temple, and a sick feeling if he ever considered interfering with its operations. Before the agents lifted the freeze command they removed any memory of their presence from the minds of their captives.

The agent's teleported back to the Temple and found Zhou waiting for them. "That didn't take long. Were you successful?"

Alice replied, "Great. We planted a suggestion in his mind that should end that problem here. If the Magistrate continues to give you trouble let us know."

Aaron said, "Zhou, before we head back to Kansas City we would appreciate something to eat to restore our energy levels."

"Oh, I think we can do better than a snack."

* * *

A year later Aaron and Alice were looking back at their achievements. Alice said, "I can't quite believe that the United Nations is going to award us their highest honor next week."

"Well, we did save their headquarters and representatives from the world governments from being blown up. Even our President is going to give us a medal for that job."

Alice snickered, "The High Priestess seemed a little miffed that the Guild didn't have a medal she could give us. Oh well, I'm sure Director Bertram will correct that oversight."

Aaron took his mate into his arms and asked, "How are you feeling? Morning sickness didn't seem as bad today."

She touched her stomach gently as a tear slowly ran down her cheek. "I'm going to get as big as a house with these twins. Mother told me that when she had Grace and me she felt the same, but experiencing it now I realize I really didn't know what she meant. At least they're not going to be identical with one being a male."

"I had a dream last night that we were chasing them as they flew around the room," Aaron said with a haunted look on his face.

"Honey! Don't say that. They're probably going to inherit our powers. Hopefully, they won't come into them until after we can prepare them for their responsible use. I didn't come into my powers until I was ten and they were weak until I was a teenager. How about you?"

"I was an early bloomer and started moving things before I could walk. Mom had to stay home with me to keep me safe until I was six, just in time for school. By then I'd learned to keep my talents a secret except to match what the other kids were doing."

"Ooh, I can see we're really going to be kept busy with two extremely gifted children. We're going to need our parents' help when they come into their powers."

"Babe, let's not borrow trouble. Maybe it's going to be a piece of cake."

"Yeah, you want to take a bet?"

* * *

Aaron and Alice returned to their apartment after the United Nations award ceremony in Paris, France. Its location was moved from New York City in 2028 after a terrorist attack leveled much of lower Manhattan. The tiny nation responsible was soon eliminated and all surviving persons who took part in the attack were brought before the World Court. Those found guilty were imprisoned for life without parole in Orbital 1.

The two honorees stood before a mirror admiring how they looked with the award around their necks. It was a Gold Sunburst Medal attached to a wide scarlet ribbon. The award also came with a small gold sunburst they were required to wear outside their quarters. This was to remind others of what they had accomplished. The award also came with other benefits, such as a special UN Passport good for entry and free lodging anywhere in the world.

Alice snickered after she struck a pose. "This is so pretentious. Our parents would laugh at us."

"Oh! I don't know, let's go to our parents and let them make that judgment," Aaron said before they teleported to his parents' home in Baltimore.

Joan gave a little start when they appeared in her living room, then smiled as she exclaimed, "Robert! They're here, come quick!" Then she ran to her son and his mate and hugged each while tears of joy ran down her cheeks. Aaron's father joined them and repeated his wife's actions, then stood back and smiled with pride at their accomplishments.

Joan quickly sought the vid recorder she'd laid out in case they came, and started recording this happy reunion. Robert said, "I mentally told Mary of your arrival and she and her family will be here shortly."

They then migrated to the kitchen table where Joan served Aaron's favorite dessert, while they waited for the rest of the family to arrive. Later, as they posed together for the family showing off their UN Award, they couldn't help tearing up a little at their families' reaction of pride.

Mary sought Alice out as she returned from the bathroom and asked, "How far along are you? Mom said you were having twins!"

"Not quite three months and according to everyone else I'm right on track. However, I'm not going to be much help to Aaron after another sixty days. Mother wants me to stay with her when I get too big to take care of myself."

Mary's face showed her concern when she replied, "I only had a single birth and I thought I was big, but with twins I can see your concern. I think your mother has the right idea. You shouldn't be left alone in that condition."

After two hours they said their goodbyes and teleported to Alice's family in Dallas. Rachel and Samuel were expecting them and had arranged for Grace, Alice's twin, to be there. It was a repeat of the reception they received from Aaron's family. After everyone had settled down, Grace wanted to know what Paris was like as she had never left Texas.

Later Alice leaned close to Grace and quietly asked, "How hard was your pregnancy with twins?"

She looked at Alice for a moment, and then taking her hand she led her to an empty bedroom and shut the door. They sat on the bed facing each other. "You're in what, the beginning of your second trimester?"

At Alice's nod, she continued, "I ended my morning sickness about this time and didn't have any trouble until the babies' increasing weight pressed on my bladder causing me to have to pee every hour, but really health-wise I had no problem except getting around because of my big belly. Mom and I will take care of you when that starts to become a problem for you, so don't worry about it."

"What problems did you have with your kids' ESP?"

"None yet, but they are only three. But as I recall, you started before me at about this time. You could always get the toy you wanted off the floor, but you shared with me."

"Yeah, I did start first. But you weren't that far behind me. Let's get back with the others before Aaron comes looking for me."

When Alice opened the bedroom door Aaron stood there with his hand raised as if to knock. Alice smiled at him and said, "Ah, there you are. I was just coming to find you and ask if you were ready to return home?"

He smiled, and then winked at her. "I'm ready when you are, but your mother wanted to take some more vid's before we left."

Alice and her mate joined hands as they moved toward the others. After taking the requested vid's and boxing up a piece of one of Alice's favorite cakes, they teleported back to Kansas City.

Arriving in their apartment they were both tired from the repeated teleportation's, so they collapsed on their couch in each other's arms and fell asleep watching a vid. Several hours later Alice awoke and persuaded Aaron to move to the more comfortable bed. The next morning Alice woke her mate to breakfast in bed.

They had just finished their shower together when they got a mental summons to join Control and the High Priestess in her quarters ASAP. Alice muttered, "Oh Crap! That means we have to change clothes when we get there and I bet we need to wear the full award as well."

Aaron said, "I think you're right and we need to tell them that your armor doesn't fit you anymore. That means you can't come with me on assignments if there's any threat of physical danger. I'm not taking any chances with you or the babies."

They soon teleported to the change room, donned their Blues and the UN Awards, then entered Director Bertram's office. She stood and inspected their attire, making minute adjustments to their uniform and Awards, before stepping back and smiling with satisfaction.

"You both look great. There's been a change in plans about your Presidential Awards. Instead of you travelling to Washington, President Elisa Gutierrez will present the Medal here within the hour. Her shuttle is on the way and she wants you two to give her a tour of the Temple afterwards. Apparently, she's curious about our organization and how it operates."

Aaron smiled at Natalie asking, "I hope you're going to lead the tour because neither of us has seen very much of the Temple's interior."

"I know. I expect what she really wants is an understanding of your personality and extra sensory gifts."

Alice grimaced before speaking, "I have a suspicion that she wants to offer us a job, something her own people can't do. Remember, I'm not 100 percent and my armor doesn't fit anymore, so you can understand why I'm wary."

Natalie shook her head, and then raised her head looking at the ceiling. "Lord, I keep forgetting you gave these two gifts to protect themselves, so why not the ability to predict the future as it applies to them. Don't worry, we aren't going to farm your abilities out unless it has a direct bearing on the Guild, and I'm not going to put you in any danger. Okay, let's meet the Priestess in her quarters until the President arrives, then we'll move to the conference room."

Aaron interrupted, "The President's shuttle is landing in our plaza now, so we better get a move on."

Natalie mentally contacted the Priestess to meet them in the conference room, where Natalie was now leading them. They met the Priestess as they arrived at their destination and entered together. Alice noted that the room's layout had changed since she was last here, probably to accommodate the Medal presentation. The three spread out behind the Priestess awaiting the President's arrival.

The first to arrive were three members of the President's Secret Service detail, followed soon by the President. She stopped before the High Priestess and gave a short bow, which was reciprocated by the Priestess. The Priestess then advanced to the President where they shook hands, then embraced each other.

They then turned and advanced on the two agents, stopping before them. The Priestess introduced each agent and Natalie as their Control. The President first shook hands with Natalie, holding her hand a little longer than usual, then turned to Aaron and Alice.

"My, you have strong extra sensory powers. You even glow a little. It's been reported that you are the strongest of anyone else in the world, is that true?"

Aaron responded, "If there are any stronger I think we would have sensed their presence."

The President nodded her head, then asked, "Besides your other abilities it's been reported that you two are the only people with the ability to teleport, is that true?"

Alice answered, "Yes, to anywhere in the world."

"That was going to be my next question. What if you needed to teleport somewhere outside this world?"

Aaron and Alice looked at each other questioningly, before Alice asked with a raised eyebrow, "Please explain what you mean exactly."

"Let's say a spaceship on the way to Mars. Can you do that?"

Aaron and Alice conferred mentally for a short time before he answered, "We haven't tried anything like that. We won't risk ourselves, but would be willing to teleport an object."

The President nodded her head, and then held up her hand saying, "Wait a moment while I confer." Then left the room.

She soon returned and stood before them chewing the inside of her mouth, then composed herself. "We have a life and death problem on the Mars spacecraft. My experts ask if you can't pull the crew off, then can you send equipment and a person there instead?"

Aaron nodded his head. "Yes, but first the equipment and then the person after its verified that the equipment arrived in good shape."

Alice interrupted, "How many people on the ship and what's their mission?"

The President looked at her in surprise. "Three and it's a resupply mission for the Mars Colony."

The two agents mentally conferred for a few minutes, then Aaron asked, "How critical is the resupply mission?"

"If we immediately sent another ship and it got there in eight months, then not critical; however, if it's delayed for any reason then people on Mars will start dying."

Alice looked into her mate's eyes until he reluctantly nodded his head. Alice turned to the President and said, "Let's send the equipment and if it's safe then the person. If they are unsuccessful in making repairs, then we will recover the crew. You better get the second ship ready in case this one can't be fixed. I'm curious if it's possible for us to teleport the supplies to Mars."

The President's face turned from concerned to a big smile as Alice spoke, then thoughtful. "What you said about you sending the supplies is something I want to pursue. After we solve this problem I want to talk to you about it again. The equipment and the person are in Houston, how soon can you get there?"

Aaron shook his head, but upon seeing Alice's grin, said, "How about this afternoon. We need a picture or a mind memory of its location."

The Medal ceremony went quickly as everyone was anxious to begin the repair or recovery of the Mars ship personnel. Aaron and Alice now had a Medal attached to a Blue Ribbon with white stars. The Medal itself was a larger version of the Medal of Honor given to military members who have proven themselves in combat at great risk to their own lives. President Gutierrez referred to their actions in saving multitudes of lives while risking their own as meeting the civilian requirements of the award.

After the ceremony President Gutierrez motioned for her Chief of Staff to join her and the medal holders. "Rachel, you've been to the Houston Space Center. These two need a picture or a memory so that they can teleport there."

Rachel thought a moment, then pulled her com devise and after punching several buttons showed the display to Alice. "Will this do the job?"

Aaron and Alice studied the display before Alice replied, "Close enough. We need to return to our apartment and change clothing. Have someone meet us at that location in twenty minutes with the authority to get this done."

President Gutierrez gave them a wide smile before answering.

"Make that forty minutes and if this works I'll owe you a big favor."

Director Bertram placed her hand on Alice's shoulder as she leaned close to her ear and whispered, "When you finish this task report back here to me."

The two agents returned to the change room, then after donning their civilian clothing they teleported back to their apartment. They placed their medals in the apartments safe before each quickly ate two energy bars and drank a liter of water in preparation for their task later today.

Checking their time they took turns taking a toilet break, then being a little anxious decided to leave a few minutes sooner than scheduled. They arrived at the Houston Space Center standing in front of the mockup of the original rockets used to send men into space. They looked around not expecting to see their greeting party, when a young female Air Force Lieutenant approached them.

"Mr. and Mrs. Pearson?"

Aaron smiled as he replied, "Yes, you must be our guide."

"Yes, I'm Lt. Jennifer Meyers and our transportation is over there." She pointed at a small shuttle sitting on the lawn. Our destination is further than the President thought, but we'll be there in about twenty minutes. They entered the shuttle and sat behind the pilot who greeted them and told them to strap in. They were soon in the air and were told their destination was west of Houston.

They were over a complex of warehouses when they descended, landing in a parking lot. A military vehicle pulled up as they left the shuttle. Six armed uniformed men quickly exited the vehicle and saluted Lt. Meyers. She looked at the agents and said, "They will be our escorts as long as you will be with us. Proceed Sergeant and we will follow."

They followed the Sergeant into a large warehouse where they immediately encountered a security checkpoint. Lt. Meyers showed her ID and handed the OIC a card that was run through a scanner, which flashed green. They then entered a maze of offices that soon opened up into a large cleared area that contained a short narrow crate.

Lt. Meyers gave Aaron a folder that contained pictures of the spacecraft, and the cargo space where the equipment crate was to be teleported. Alice asked the Lieutenant, "Have you informed the crew what we intend to do?"

"Wait a moment. It takes a little time to communicate with them." She then used her com and queried someone about the ship's reply. After a moment she got her answer and thanked the other party. "Yes, they were doubtful, but agreed to stay clear of the area and report if the equipment arrives in good shape."

"For my own information, just how far is the ship from Earth?"

"About 31,500,000 kilometers."

Aaron and Alice looked at the picture of the cargo area of the space ship until they were sure it was imprinted in their merged minds and then visualized the crate there. There was a slight pop as the crate vanished amid surprised intakes of breathe from the others in the room.

Lt. Meyers spoke into her com, "It's on its way!"

While they were waiting for confirmation Aaron was looking around the large open area wondering what all those crates and boxes contained. Ten minutes later Lt. Meyers received a call, then looking at the couple she held up her thumb. "It made it there in good shape!"

CHAPTER FOURTEEN

Aaron asked Lt. Meyers, "Where is the person to be teleported?"

"He's on his way here. Do you need any snacks to build your strength before you teleport him?"

"Do you have any energy bars?"

"Sergeant, do you or any of your men have some?"

"Men! Dig out any you are carrying."

Every man in the group had at least one bar, which was taken by the Sergeant and given to the Lieutenant, who gave the eight bars to Aaron. "We'll take four and the men can have the others back."

Aaron and Alice were eating when a man wearing an Air Force jump suit arrived accompanied by three armed uniformed men. "Aaron and Alice Pearson this Captain Richard Eagan. He's the one you're going to send to the space ship."

They shook Captain Eagan's hand and then studied him. He seemed cool and undisturbed by what they were going to try. Aaron asked, "You are aware that we haven't tried to send a human into space before?"

His eyes got bigger in surprise before he blurted, "You did send my equipment box there okay?"

"Yes, but that's not the same as an organic being. Alice, what do you place the odds of this working?"

"Oh, a little better than fifty percent, maybe sixty percent. I'm anxious to see if this works before I try it."

Captain Eagan's face turned white as he realized this was much more dangerous than he realized. Then his face cleared suddenly as he realized his leg was being pulled - hard. "Damn you! What are the real odds?"

Aaron smiled at him. "Ninety plus, but this is still the first time we've tried this at this distance and through space."

"Okay, how far have you teleported in the past?"

"Anywhere on Earth, never off Earth except that equipment crate. However, if we got that there then you should make it too."

"Okay I'm ready if you are. Let's get this done before it gets further away."

Alice asked, "How about your tools?"

"Hopefully they're already on-board inside the crate."

Aaron and Alice merged their minds, picturing Captain Eagan beside the crate inside the ship, then wished him there. There was a slight pop when he disappeared.

Lt. Meyers spoke into her com. "He's left! Check the time here and when he arrives."

Aaron looked at Alice and shook his head. "It should be instantaneous."

Ten minutes later Lt. Meyers com beeped, after getting the message she smiled and held up her thumb. "He made it and said that's the only way to travel. Before you leave we need you to send additional supplies to the ship because of the extra man on board."

After sending the supplies they teleported to Director Bertram's office. She looked up as they appeared and gazed at them for a moment before motioning them to sit. "How did it go?"

Alice gave her a small smile before replying, "It went well. It appears that extreme distance is not a problem for us, at least not so far. What about the President's plan for us to teleport supplies directly to the Mars Colony?"

"I've discussed that with the Priestess and we agreed to offer your services once a month in exchange for publicity for your actions. It puts you two in the news regularly helping mankind and saving lives."

Aaron thoughtfully said, "We can also offer to return people to Earth for emergency medical treatment."

"Yes, that's a good point. I bet that would be a good morale boast for the colony knowing that they had a way of getting help in an emergency. I'll ask the President about this and other matters when I talk to her when we next meet. You two have done excellent work and deserve some time off to recharge, so take a week off. If I need you I'll let you know."

The first two days of their vacation they did very little except housekeeping chores and physical exercise. The second evening Alice snuggled up against her mate on the couch and said softly, "I'm bored. Let's do something tomorrow, something away from here, something exciting!" Then she playfully bit his ear lobe. "I'll make it worthwhile," she said in a sexy voice.

"Well, we could go to Mars and sit in the Sun."

"Not that exciting! I was thinking maybe lying on a Hawaii beach in the Sun. I could play tricks on the women who give you the eye."

"As long as you make it worthwhile to me. What do I get?"

Alice whispered softly in his ear, then ran toward the bedroom with Aaron close on her heels.

* * *

Five years later Alice was sure she was going to have a nervous breakdown. Laura and David were mentally playing dodge ball and she was the target. Finally having enough of her kids' antics she removed their ammunition and put them in time out, placing them under an overturned playpen. So far they couldn't use their powers to escape and just sat there with glum faces looking at her.

"Listen you two, if you can't behave then you stay there. Let me know what your decision is going to be."

Alice went to the adjoining kitchen and started preparing lunch while silently following the mental thoughts of her children. Laura was the troublemaker and the dominant personality of the two. She was also strong willed, but Alice knew her weakness as she set a bowl of chocolate ice cream on the counter where they both could see it. Alice could hear Laura's thoughts change from stubbornness to desire as she looked at the ice cream.

Mommy, we're sorry. If we agree to be good can we have

some of that ice cream?

"I don't know. You were very mean to me and you really hurt my feelings."

We won't do that anymore. Pleeease!

"David! How about you?"

Ohh mommy we were just having fun. I'll be good.

"Okay. But, if you act bad again no ice cream for a week!"

Alice mentally raised the playpen, releasing the children who ran to the kitchen table and sat quietly while Alice placed a small bowl of ice cream in front of them. "Remember, act good and you get ice cream, bad and you get time out."

They both mentally said, *Yes Mommy.*

While her children were eating she thought, *they are about four and a half years old and should be talking with their audible voices. Maybe it's because they don't need to because Aaron and I can hear their mental voices. Next year they are going to start school at the Temple and their teachers are going to demand they use their audible voices. I'll talk to Aaron when he returns tonight.*

That evening Aaron appeared in their bedroom and quickly made his way to where his family were watching a vid. "Hey kids, don't I get a welcome?"

David and Laura ran to their father mentally screaming their welcome. He picked them up and carried them to the couch where they hugged his neck and mentally asked where he had been and if he had brought them anything.

"Well, let me check and see if I have something." Aaron then pulled a small Eiffel Tower out of a pocket and handed it to David, who quickly moved to the floor to play with it. Looking at Laura he started patting his pockets as if looking for something until she said, "Oh Daddy, it's in this pocket." Pointing at his jacket pocket.

"Well, well. I think you're right. What do I have here?"

"Oh, oh. You brought me a little doll!" She said before he pulled it out of his pocket and gave it to her.

Aaron and Alice sat together and observed their children playing. Alice mentally said, *I was worried that the kids were not audibly speaking, but at least Laura is capable.*

He responded, *did you catch that Laura knew what her gift was before I showed it to her?*

Yes, and she knew what pocket it was in too. I couldn't do that at her age. We better take her and David to the Temple for testing. We may have a budding precognition ability here. That's a really rare ESP ability.

The next day the Pearson family teleported to the change room next to Director Bertram's office. After changing into their Blues they entered Natalie's office. Her eyes widened in surprise when the children followed the agents into the office.

"Well, who have we here? Is this Laura and David and what brings them here?"

Alice mentally prodded her children, who responded in unison, "Hello Director Bertram."

When Natalie raised an eyebrow, Aaron said, "They need to be tested to determine their abilities."

"Very well, but return here after you drop them off at the Testing Center for a debriefing on your last assignment."

Thirty minutes later they were back in the Director's office. Natalie leaned back in her chair and regarded her two agents. "What's happened?"

Alice frowned as she considered then shrugged her shoulders. "Laura is the strong one and David follows her lead. She was the first to show her abilities and remains stronger than her brother. Now she may show Precognition ability, or she may simply be reading our minds. In any case we need to be aware of what she and David can do."

"Precog ability! That would be helpful in your work to know what's going to happen in the future. I assume this ability hasn't occurred in either of your families before?"

Aaron shrugged his shoulders. "I was the first person to have teleportation powers, so I'm not surprised if our kids have something new in addition to our powers. We won't know how strong their powers are going to be until they get older, maybe another ten-fifteen years."

Alice shook her head. "I have a feeling that it's not going to be that long for our kids. These are not normal Guild children."

Natalie smiled. "So says an impartial parent. But you're right, we do need to know what their gifts are, how strong they are now, and what their potential strength will be. Aaron, tell me about your last assignment."

An hour later they were discussing humorous aspects of some

of their past experiences when Aaron and Alice received a mental notification that the testing was completed. They quickly said their goodbyes and headed toward the Testing Center.

The testing supervisor met them at the door and appeared stressed as she ushered them into her office. "Before I show you the results of the testing be aware that the Priestess has placed a nondisclosure ban on the findings."

When seated she displayed the results on a vid screen. Alice gripped her mate's hand as they viewed the screen. Laura's results were higher than David's by at least ten percent, but they both shared the same talents including teleportation. What got their attention was they both had healing powers.

Aaron asked, "What about Precognition, that's not listed?"

"That power is so rare that we haven't yet developed a reliable test. You don't seem surprised that your children both test as Reds, why is that?"

Alice interrupted, "That information is considered secret by order of the Priestess. Please put a seal on these test results until the Priestess releases them. Thank you for your consideration. Would you now bring the children out and we will leave."

Laura and David were soon brought to them and the family returned to Director Bertram's office. Once inside Alice gave Natalie a hard copy of the test results. After reviewing the results she looked at the parents with a raised eyebrow. "Alice, you were right. These results are not those of normal Guild children. No mention is made of Precognition?"

"They say that the tests for that aren't reliable, so I'll look for that power on my own. It also appears we passed the healing power to our kids, but all their powers are weak because they are only four and a half. I think Laura is going to be the strong one when they mature."

"I told the Priestess you were here with the children and she wants to see all of you in her quarters."

Aaron looked at Alice in surprise before saying, "Now? Is she sure, because sometimes our kids are like half tamed savages."

Natalie gave Laura and David a stern look, who looked back at her with innocent faces and slowly smiled. "Yes, I see what you mean, but you may be surprised. Okay, everyone follow me."

The Priestess bid them to enter at their knock and everyone

followed Natalie into the presence of the High Priestess. Aaron was holding David's hand, while Alice tightly gripped Laura's. The Priestess smiled at the children and mentally said, *Laura, David have you been instructed about your family's history?*

They both replied by shaking their heads that they hadn't. *Please follow me I want to show you a painting of the person from which you have descended.*

They followed her to a painting of a woman with white hair. *Her name is Angel Pearson. She lived over 200 years ago and started the line we now call The Healing Guild. God gave her healing gifts that have been passed down to the members of the Guild. He has been kind and has given even greater powers to your parents and now you. Your powers were given so that you could assist your parents when you mature. In the meantime you must train yourselves to be ready when the time is right. You both have the ability to heal by touch, a gift that only female Reds normally have. You cannot share this knowledge outside your immediate family. You will eventually be able to teleport, a power that no one besides your parents have. Do not attempt to use this power without one of your parents. Laura can you or David tell what is going to happen in the future?*

Laura looked guiltily at her mother before replying, "Yes Priestess, I knew we were going to see the Angel painting." David said, "Me too."

Very good! This is a power your parents don't have and will be useful when you work with them. Did you know that every High Priestess takes the name of Angel Pearson to honor our founder? You should honor your founder by working hard to be ready when it is your turn to protect the Guild. Do either of you have questions?

Laura eagerly stepped forward and asked, "Did you say we have greater powers than our founder?"

"Yes, you should study your ancestor. She also had a Guardian Angel and a Messenger Angel. Her Messenger Angel has reappeared and talked with your parents. This is her first appearance in over 200 years. I have a feeling that you two will see her when the time is right. Any more questions? Well, if you want to talk with me have your parents make an appointment."

The Pearson family went back to the change room, then after

donning civilian clothing teleported back to their apartment. Once there Alice took the hands of her children and led them to their living room couch where she sat and had them stand in front of her.

"Laura, David do you have questions for your father or me?"

Laura looked at her twin for a moment, nodded her head, and then asked, "Momma, why haven't you told us about our family history? Is it because you thought we were too young to understand?"

Alice looked at her mate and shrugged her shoulders. "Kids, we didn't realize you were mature enough to understand your heritage and responsibility, the way you were acting before certainly didn't indicate that degree of maturity."

Laura rolled her eyes at her mother. "Momma, we were playing and got a little carried away. Now we know what we are going to be doing with our lives and that's a lot more interesting than playing dodge ball with you. Tell us what you want us to do and we will try our best to do it."

Aaron sat beside Alice and said, "Very well, this sounds more like the maturity we were looking for. We are going to place you in pre-school where you will have close contact with other Guild children. Most or all these children will not be as advanced as you two. We want you to go undercover about your abilities."

David interrupted, "You mean like a secret agent like you and momma?"

Aaron smiled. "A little. Don't show any abilities that the other kids haven't already used and don't show your full strength. If someone gets hurt don't use your healing powers, instead ask a Blue to call for a Red to take care of the injury if the Blue can't help. Don't use your ability to teleport unless one of us is present. We don't want to go to Mars to bring you back, besides you would die up there without air to breathe. Any questions?"

With a serious expression Laura asked, "You and momma dress as a Blue when you go to see Natalie, but you both have healing powers of a Red. Do some other men have healing powers?"

Alice responded, "No, only your father and David. We don't know why God has given only them this power. It is something you are not to reveal to others unless we give our approval. If you encounter a child wearing Red clothing be friendly but not so close that they might guess your healing power. As you mature and your powers grow stronger others can sense that you are powerful without you ever demonstrating your abilities. Learn how to mingle without calling attention to yourselves, be a secret agent."

Alice gazed into her children's eyes and mentally read their surface thoughts as she saw and felt their excitement as they pictured themselves in this new role. "Okay, any more questions?"

David excitedly asked, "So we are going to dress as Blues when we attend school?"

"Yes, I recently got some. I want you to try them on and see if they fit properly."

Soon the children returned dressed in their school uniform, much like what an adult Blue would wear except theirs had a tracker if they became separated from others in their class. Alice adjusted Laura's tunic while Aaron checked the fit of David's clothing. Alice had the children stand side-by-side and slowly smiled. "Yes, they look like any other Blue kids. It will be a good disguise as you learn how to be a secret agent."

Laura said, "Momma, except for her white hair you look exactly like Angel Pearson. I know all the Guild women look alike, but you really look like her. Do you know why that is?"

"I don't know, but God must have a reason for making us look alike. Maybe you will look like her as well."

"Oh, I hope so. She's very beautiful, just like you Momma."

CHAPTER FIFTEEN

Eight years later Laura and David were waiting at the Temple School for one of their parents to pick them up and they were late. Laura was beginning to worry, as they were never late, so she tried to reach her mother mentally. She had never tried this before when her parents were not in her presence.

Mom! We are waiting for you at school.

Oh honey, we are dealing with an emergency. Ask Natalie to sit with you and David until we can get back.

Okay Mom, see you soon.

Natalie, this is Laura. Mom and Dad are dealing with a problem and ask that you watch over us until they get back. We are at the Temple School.

I'll be right there.

When Natalie arrived at the school she found the twins sitting on a bench studying together on a math assignment. Looking up, Laura smiled at Natalie as she approached. "Hi Natalie, thanks for sitting with us."

"That's alright I wanted to talk to you and David anyway."

When they reached her office she had them take a seat while she leaned forward in her chair and observed how much they had grown. At twelve they were starting to look like the adults they were soon going to be. Laura appeared to be a younger Alice, while David was in a growth spurt that made him two inches taller than his twin.

"David, who in your family do you look like?"

"Dad thinks I look like Uncle Jason, his sister's first born. But, I think I've got Dad's nose and ears."

Natalie smiled at that response. "Laura, whose idea was it to have me sit for you and David?"

"Mom, after I mentally called her to ask what was the delay in picking us up."

"Did you know that they were in Calcutta, India?"

"Wow, that's a long way off. I've never done that before," Laura exclaimed excitedly.

"Yes, not many Blues can use telepathy at that distance. I'd guess you now have your parents' power. I wonder if your other gifts have matured?"

An hour later Aaron and Alice teleported into Natalie's office. They smiled as their children jumped up from their chairs and ran to hug them. Later, after the greetings were over, Alice took Laura aside and asked, "Honey, is that the first time you've used telepathy when the party you're talking to is not present?"

"Yes Mom. I did it with no effort. Natalie told me later that you were in Calcutta. Does this mean we've come into our powers?"

"Probably. Tomorrow you don't have school, so we're going to experiment. David, are you and Laura excited?"

The twins looked at each other with eyes gleaming with expectation as they nodded their heads. The following morning they teleported to a small uninhabited island. They all looked around at the white sand beaches and palm trees waving in the ocean breeze, so much different than the cold weather of Kansas City. Aaron and Alice sought shade while the children enjoyed the surf.

A short time later they called the children to join them. Alice asked, "What should we test first?"

Aaron smiled mischievously as he mentally said, *David, try to read the surface thoughts of Natalie without her knowledge.*

He and Alice mentally followed David's attempt, as first he found her mind glow and then gradually entered her surface thoughts until it was clear that she was wondering how the Pearson children were doing. David immediately withdrew and slammed shut their entry into his thoughts. David looked their way and smiled as he enjoyed his success.

Alice smiled at her son. "That was well done. Who taught you how to shield your thoughts?"

"Laura, shortly after we started school. Some of the other kids were testing their telepathy skills on their classmates so we learned how to block them. We tested several methods on each other until we found one that no one was able to break."

Aaron thought a moment then asked, "Since you two have been testing each other, who do you consider the strongest?"

"Well, so far Laura is slightly stronger than me in telepathy and psychokinesis, but neither of us wanted to try to control fire. I know you where interested in our abilities in precognition, but while we both occasionally see scenes from the future we don't do it on demand, which is the whole point of it being useful."

Alice grimaced. "Yeah, you're right."

"Laura, we are going to try to do two tests, one your ability to tell the future and two your ability to teleport. How about you and David think hard on where we are going to teleport, which is the living room of our apartment. Picture a spot firmly in your mind, then wish yourself there. When you're ready do it."

There were two soft pops as they disappeared, then Aaron and Alice teleported to their bedroom. They could hear their children laugh with joy as they realized how easy it was. When they entered the living room their children ran to them and hugged them. Laura said, "What a rush, but I didn't get a future vision."

"Neither did I," said David.

Aaron looked at his mate. "I wonder if they could do it if they mind merged?"

"Maybe, but remember we were mated when we did it. That's pretty intimate stuff for a brother and sister to do."

"Yes, but Angel and Alice mind merged and they were mother and daughter. Angel's Alice was about the same age as our Laura."

Alice grimaced. "Let's not do anything that we're not sure will be safe at their age. As they mature further this question may become moot. Is there another test we should be considering?"

"I don't know, kids is there some power where you think you're weak?"

At their negative response, Alice said, "Let's go to Paris for lunch. Kids go change into something nice and we'll do the same."

* * *

Five years later the family were together in London on assignment. This was Laura and David's first time working with their parents. The twins had matured into strong young adults, Laura a younger version of her beautiful mother and David a handsome tall muscular young man.

Before this assignment the twins were fitted with armor, much like the silks their parents wore. They were following the mental thoughts of a person who was plotting against one of the Reds working at the local Temple. The twins were carrying Temple Passports while their parents were using their UN passports in the event they had to supply the police with ID's.

They were standing in front of a hotel that Aaron and Alice had used previously and were taking a directional reading of the signal they were receiving, when Laura pointed a finger westward. "I make it west by southwest about eight kilometers."

Aaron spoke, "Does everyone agree?"

At their mental acknowledgement he hailed two robo cabs, the men taking one and the women the other travelling at a slight angle either side of the line indicated by Laura. When the cabs traveled about eight kilometers they each stopped and took another reading. David mentally reported, *I feel the person is to my right about two blocks.* Laura reported, *My reading is a block to my left. We are getting out of the cab here and will meet you at the location of the source.*

The men and the women soon converged outside an older eight-story apartment building. David said, "The source is on the third floor, toward the rear."

Laura said, "I agree. Now what do we do?"

Aaron said, "For the moment let's listen and try to learn his or her plans."

Laura blurted out, "It's a he as he just walked by a mirror and checked himself out."

Alice said, "David describe him to us."

"He appears to be about my height based upon his reflection, dark brown hair cut in the style favored here, light brown jacket with an arm band of a soccer team, his face has no markings and is clean shaven."

"Laura it's your turn, anything else?"

"I agree on the height, he would be attractive to a woman, and I caught a glimpse of a hat in his hand as he moved away from the mirror."

Aaron said, "You two face the door while we have our backs to him when he comes out. Don't look at him directly, use your hands when talking to us and laugh as if someone said something funny, but don't overdo it."

Soon their source left the building and headed toward a nearby pub on their side of the street. They waited a few minutes before following him and took a table where they could observe him sitting at the bar. When a woman joined him they moved to a table near where the family was sitting. The source and the woman almost immediately started to argue and as it became heated it became easy to hear what they were saying.

"Robert, I don't care if she's a healer. I'm not going to play second fiddle to another woman. You drop her or I'm out of here!"

"Lilly don't be so sensitive. You know I love you and I'm only seeing her so I can convince her to heal my brother of AIDS. No one must know or he'll lose his mate and his job! That bitch he's hooked up with is real piece of work."

The woman glared at Robert with clinched fists as she spit out, "If you don't get rid of Erica by this time tomorrow then we're quits."

She left her chair in such a rush that it fell to the floor with a crash, startling everyone who then watched her stomp out of the Pub. Robert watched her leave with a stricken face, then gulped down his beer and followed her out of the Pub.

A wait staff appeared to take their order and Aaron ordered the daily lunch special, less the beer. David raised his eyebrow at his father who replied, "I know you're of age, but you would have been carded and I want us to stay undercover. When we finish eating we'll go to the Temple and talk to Erica."

After lunch they found an alley out of sight and teleported to the front entrance of the London Temple. The family approached the reception desk, but before Aaron could state his business the receptionist said, "Mr. Pearson do you need to see the Security Head?"

"Oh, you remember me. Yes, we need to speak with security."

Less than a minute later two big men approached them. One of the men said, "Mr. Pearson my name is Joseph Taylor and we will escort you to Security Head Mary Ann Hicks."

Hicks was standing behind her desk as they were ushered into the room. "Ah, Aaron and Alice we meet again. I hope it's not another disaster involving our Temple. What can we do for you?"

"No, this is more a PR problem and I wanted you to meet our children. Laura, David this is Mary Ann Hicks who has helped us a number of times and you may need her help as well in the future."

"So your team has expanded and this is their first mission? My Alice, she looks like a younger version of you and David is going to be a heart breaker. I bet they have all your powers too. We may need them the way things keep coming apart. What can I do for you?"

Alice smiled at Mary Ann and shook her head. "I see you have another hunk for your Second. Is he good at his job?"

"Yes, I only pick the good ones. The previous one is now Head of Security at the Dublin Temple."

"We need to interview a Red by the name of Erica. Hopefully, there are not too many with that name."

Mary Ann consulted her tablet and said, "We have two, one is twenty-six and the other is forty-eight."

"Let's try the younger one first. Would you see if she's available and set us up with an interview room."

"You're in luck. She's free until two o'clock. If you like I can put the two young ones in an adjacent room with a one-way glass to observe you in action."

"Yes, that would be perfect. Too many people asking questions is counterproductive in this instance."

Fifteen minutes later Erica was escorted into the interview room. Aaron introduced themselves and asked the Red to take a seat and relax. "You may have heard of us since we have been in the news as trouble shooters for the High Priestess. We are here because we have heard mental thoughts from someone named Robert thinking about a Red named Erica. We have reason to believe he may use force to make you use your powers to heal his brother. Are you that Erica?"

"You can do that? Just pull up thoughts from anywhere in the world! You must really be powerful."

Erica's face showed her distress before placing her hands over her eyes and bowing her head while silently crying, her misery overwhelming their senses. "Robert, what are you thinking!" She loudly cried out."

She raised her head, tears running down her cheeks. In a passion filled voice she said, "I told him we are governed by rules in order to be fair to all who seek our help. What he wanted me to do is forbidden and I refused. He won't accept that and keeps after me. See my arm, these bruises are from our last meeting."

Alice said, "Look at me!"

Startled, Erica looked into her eyes. "You must stop seeing this man. He is a user and has another lover who may come after you as well. You deserve someone who loves you as you are and respects your obligations. If this continues we may have to take action against him. Do you want that?"

Erica looked at Alice and knew instantly that she threatened her lover with a partial mind wipe. "No! I promise to never see him again. He won't be a threat anymore, I promise."

"Very well, but you know we will be watching Robert to see if he's a threat. Now, take the remainder of the day off and compose yourself before seeing another patient."

Erica rose from her seat and ran to Alice hugging her before leaving the room. After Erica left Aaron asked, "Do you think she will do it?"

"Yes, she's afraid of what we'll do to Robert if she doesn't. Now let's see what our kids' reactions are going to be."

CHAPTER SIXTEEN

Later that evening as they were finishing their dinner, Aaron spoke to his children. "We need to have a discussion about your future. You both did very well at your first outing as agents; however, before we continue your mother and I think you should consider whether to continue with us or start medical school for a career as a Blue. We want to hear your thoughts and desires."

Laura looked at her parents and gave a little snort of laughter. "Do you actually think we would prefer a career as a Red or Blue when we could do what we did today. It would be boring for us. We were born to do this, otherwise we wouldn't have been given these extra powers by God."

Suddenly, they were joined by a beautiful women wearing clothing from a past age. Alice gasped, "Barbara!"

"My your children are terrific, especially Laura. So quick on the up-take and she looks remarkably like us. I think she's even prettier."

Laura, whose mouth was open in surprise at Barbara's appearance, quickly smiled at the angel. "We appear to be about the same age, so it must be my hair style that is the difference. Mother, what do you think?"

Barbara started to laugh, and then quickly covered her mouth. "See! I haven't had a laugh like that since Angel was alive, I do miss her. But let's get to the point of my arrival. These two would be wasted doing anything else. However, if you insist they be given their choice so be it. Laura, David what is it to be?"

They said in unison, "Agents!"

"Well, that's it then. Now your power to see into the future is activated by thinking **Future** before you start an assignment. You will then have a quick preview of what will happen. After you use it a few times it will become second nature. You were given healing powers in case one or more of your family is gravely injured while working for God. Any questions?"

David shyly smiled. "How are we going to find mates if we are not part of the Temple population?"

"Eventually you each will be assigned a powerful mate when the time is right, much like your parents were. Anything else?"

Alice frowned at Barbara, then said, "They need at least two more years of training before sending them out to train their mates."

"They could do it now, they are very smart and capable individuals. First, I must find them the right mates. If you need me I am close at hand."

When Barbara disappeared, Laura grabbed Alice's arm. "Mom, let's go to the bedroom!"

When they were in the bedroom and the door shut, Laura passionately asked, "What did Barbara mean when she said she would find us mates much like you and Dad?"

Laura looked into her daughter's eyes and found herself two decades earlier. "When we started Natalie brought together Aaron and me as the two most powerful Blues in the world. Later, as we were getting to know each other and our abilities we started talking to each other mentally. Your father's mental touch caused me to have a huge sexual reaction toward him, one that I had a hard time controlling. We thought our partnership was doomed until Barbara appeared and told us that what we were feeling was love for each other that would abate to controllable levels once we mated. She may mean that's what will happen to you if the man she picks is compatible to you."

"Did Dad feel the same urges as you?"

"Yes, but not as strongly until we actually mated. Be sure you're not wearing armor when you first try a mental conversation."

"You think!! You better warn David, I'm not sure about his ability to control his emotions."

"I already passed that on to Aaron. They are in the other bedroom now. Honey, is this revelation disturbing? Talk to me."

"I've wondered about your courtship, how you mated so soon after meeting. That isn't how other Blues meet and court before they mate. God ordained this mating. I know you and Dad still love each other so I'm not frightened that my selected mate will not suit me emotionally. You and Dad both continue to receive admiring looks from the opposite sex and I'm sure my mate will suit me in all respects."

"Honey, you and your brother normally wouldn't have a problem getting a mate; however, finding one that meets our ESP requirements is the rub. I hope Barbara finds mates that speak English."

Laura slowly smiled, then said, "I could always learn his language and we could mentally talk with each other until I'm proficient."

"That would mean we would have to learn a new language too!"

"Ah Mom, you already speak two, what's one more."

* * *

Two years later Laura and David teleported into Natalie's office to give their official action report on their successful assignment in Bombay, India. Laura began, "A Hindu splinter group kidnapped five Blues demanding the local Temple leave the city. We followed the mind traces of the Blues and teleported into the building where they were being held and quickly froze the kidnappers and released the hostages. After the kidnappers were turned over to the police and statements given, we returned the Blues to the Temple."

Natalie asked David, "Anything she missed?"

"Well, there were fifteen hostiles in the building and they started firing projectile weapons at us as soon as we appeared. We each deployed a force shield around us to stop the projectiles, but Laura took a hit in the butt before we got the shields up."

"Laura, were you injured?"

"No, just my pride. The silks stopped the projectile, but it still stung."

"Well done, you both have performed well since you've been on your own. This is what, your tenth mission since your parents cut you loose?"

David nodded his head before saying, "That's right, do we get a party?"

"No, I have a surprise for you two. The angel Barbara has found possible mates for each of you."

The twins eyes widened in surprise as two Blues entered the office. "Laura and David Pearson meet James Blake and Lucy Tomasi. Mr. Blake is from the Greater LA Metro of southern California and Ms. Tomasi is from Tokyo, Japan. They both have high psi talents, not as high as yours but sufficient for this meeting. They have been informed of whom you are, your parents, and that they are possible mates for you. We have provided two apartments for this initial meeting in the same building where you now reside. Here are the key cards with the room numbers. I wish you good luck."

Laura and David each took a card and then Laura motioned the two Blues to follow them into the change room where they took charge of their potential mate and teleported to their apartment building lobby. The two Blues both gasped in surprise gripping the twins tightly before stepping back.

Lucy said, "We teleported!! Nobody can do that, yet you have that ability."

Laura smiled at them. "James you come with me and Lucy you're with David. We'll explain what's going on and later we have a decision to make."

They took an elevator to their separate floors and entered their rooms. Laura led James to a couch were they sat facing each other. "Obviously Natalie didn't give you complete information about us. Our parents and we can teleport anywhere on Earth and perhaps further, we can use telepathy to anywhere on Earth and have all the other psi powers. What are your psi powers?"

James gave her a small smile before shaking his head. "I thought I had strong telepathy and the ability to move objects, but your powers are awesome."

"Do you have an attraction to me? Do you think I'm pretty?"

"You're the most beautiful woman I've ever met. All the Temple women look alike, but you seem to glow."

"I think you're handsome, so we're physically attracted to each other. Don't do this yet, but when we converse mentally, if we're compatible then we'll each have a compulsion to have sexual relations. Your compulsion should not be as strong as mine, so please break the connection if I try to attack you."

"How do you know about this sexual compulsion?"

"My mother and father went through this before they mated. The angel Barbara said this was a test of their love for each other."

"The angel Barbara! Your family is the one visited by her. Oh my, God is directing your path. Wait a moment so I can think."

He looked at the most beautiful woman he had ever met then gave himself a mental kick.

"Okay I'm ready if you are."

Laura gave James a shy smile before he entered her mind. *Is this what you want?*

Immediately she felt a strong physical attraction that grew stronger as he was in her mind. *James withdraw before I attack you. I can hardly restrain myself.*

James withdrew and Laura visibly relaxed as she exhaled. "I've never had such an attraction toward another man before. How about you?"

"My attraction was strong, but I was able to control it. What now?"

"Do you have a girlfriend or arrangement of some kind with a girl?"

"No. How about you?"

"Same here. The next step is mating. How do you feel about that?"

"Wow! That's a big step. We haven't even courted."

"Remember, God has given us a test to see if we are compatible and we have passed that test. The next step is mating unless you aren't ready to commit."

James looked into the eyes of this beautiful woman and said with a choked voice, "Let's do it!"

"First I have to remove my armor, stay here while I take care of that. No, you will have to know about this part too." She removed her clothing and appeared to be nude until she released the tab and started pulling the armor off until she stood naked before him.

"Wow! You are the most fantastic woman I've ever known."

He then quickly shed his clothing until he too was naked. Laura took his hand and led him into the bedroom where they stood and admired each other's bodies. She entered his mind and it seemed to melt as they merged into one being. They fell onto the bed and made frantic love to each other until something seemed to explode within their bodies. They lay together regaining their strength and then they again made love until they couldn't move, lying entangled together on the bed.

She poked her lover in the ribs with her finger trying to get more action out of him. Giving up she got out of bed looking for food before realizing this wasn't her apartment. Laura teleported to her kitchen and retrieved several energy bars and while eating one thought of Lucy. She traced Lucy's mind glow and found her awake in the same condition. "Lucy, this is Laura. Meet me in your living room and I'll give you some energy bars. My guy pooped out too."

She then teleported to the living room using Lucy's memory. It wasn't long before Lucy made her way into the room. The two naked women looked at each other, then Lucy smiled. "Your brother is an excellent lover, but no staying power. Yours knocked out too?"

"Yeah, here's some energy bars. We keep them when we do a lot of teleporting and need quick energy. It might bring them around. It's worth a try. Later, tell David to meet in our old apartment to make plans for our mating announcements, say about six and we'll go out for dinner."

"Okay. Did anyone ever tell you that you look like Angel Pearson?"

"Yeah, the High Priestess who has a painting of Angel by her sister Elizabeth, said Mother looked like Angel and I look like my mother."

"Oh my, we're going to need to talk about this further. See you later."

Later as arranged by Laura, they met at the twins' apartment. Both of the men looked exhausted while Laura and

Lucy appeared normal. Laura shook her head at the men before smiling at her new sister-in-law. "What wimps these guys are. Lucy since you've mated with my brother you must have gone through the initiation. Do your psi powers feel stronger? Try using your telepathy with your parents in Japan."

Lucy looked at Laura in surprise, and then her face reflected a look of astonishment. After a minute Lucy took a big breath, "What happened? The longest distance I could do before was less than 1,000 kilometers!"

"According to Mother, when we initially mate the weaker partner receives the same abilities of the other. Which means you should be able to teleport now as well as having stronger existing powers. Mother and Dad had more than one upgrade, each preceded by extreme sexual activity. Apparently this is God's method of upgrading our abilities."

James and Lucy looked at each other in wonder before Lucy softly said, "You mean we were handpicked by God to be your mates?"

"Actually, Barbara did the selection, but that's nitpicking."

"By Barbara you mean the angel Barbara don't you?"

"Yes. It's likely our Messenger Angel Barbara will visit us all. She reappeared before our parents mated. We are direct descendants of Angel Pearson and that is our tie to Barbara. Let's go eat. I've made reservations at a nice restaurant and we can discuss how we are going to handle the Mating Ceremony."

CHAPTER SEVENTEEN

The next day they were all in Natalie's office. She looked at the group and smiled. "Well, I see that you've all mated. Do you newbie's have a handle on your new psi abilities?"

Lucy proudly answered, "We teleported here on our own and we both have greatly improved telepathy powers."

Natalie studied the new pair for a moment before saying, "The Pearson's all have the ability to heal, which probably has been passed on to you. Barbara said this was done in order for any of you to heal someone in your group of severe injuries. Do not reveal this power to anyone else; it might adversely affect the Red/Blue relationship since all Reds are female. Our agents are undercover and are required to wear Blues when inside the Temple. Your mate will inform you of our rules and I see you have brought civilian clothes with you - good! What plans have you made for your mating ceremony?"

David said, "We have decided to teleport to each of our mate's parents to introduce ourselves and make plans, so this is going to take awhile. Mom and Dad are going to be our first visit so that they can handle any assignments later."

"Good! Once you've trained your mates we'll have three sets of agents to handle the workload. Take off and let me know about the ceremony because I'll want to attend, maybe the Priestess as well."

Laura had mentally informed her parents they were coming, so it wasn't a surprise when they appeared inside the apartment. Alice closely appraised her children's mates; James Blake was a handsome, tall muscular man with sandy colored hair and stood beside his mate holding her hand. Lucy Tomasi was of obvious Japanese descent, but due to her taller height and Eurasian features she must have had a Caucasian mother, and was very beautiful. David had his arm around her shoulders and both her children were proud and very much in love with their mates.

Alice smiled at everyone. "So Barbara came through with her promise for your mates and I can see that you're very much in love with each other. Now comes the planning for the ceremony. With twins, that doubles the problems and with Lucy…Where are your parents located?"

David answered. "Tokyo. We're going their next and then to Greater LA Metro for James' parents."

Aaron said, "Don't forget about your grandparents in Baltimore and Dallas. I know they would want to attend. Did Natalie say anything about wanting to attend?"

Laura frowned as she replied, "Yes we need to add her to our list and she mentioned that the Priestess may want to as well."

Aaron said, "Wait! She attended by vid at our ceremony, which substantially added to the attendance. When selecting the venue that will be a big factor."

Alice interrupted. "Girls we need to consider the wedding dress. Laura you may use mine, which is quite old, so be very careful with it. I think it will fit you, but you need to try it on. Lucy how about you?"

"I don't know. I need to ask Mother when we get there. May I mentally consult with you after we arrive there?"

Alice hugged her. "You can talk to me anytime. You're one of mine now so don't be shy."

The women went to where the wedding dress was stored and carefully opened the box, slowly removing the protective covering. The young women gasped in wonder as the dress was revealed. Alice said, "This wedding dress is over 170 years old and has come down to me as the last in the family getting married. I'll pass it on the same way."

Laura tried the wedding dress on and found it fit her perfectly. Alice shook her head in wonder. "Lucy, look at us. We're like two peas in a pod."

"Yes, like two Angel Pearson's. God works his magic in mysterious ways."

Later, they said their goodbyes and teleported to Tokyo. Lucy had made arrangements with her parents, who were both Blues, to meet in their apartment. However, she had forgotten to mention they were teleporting. When they suddenly appeared her mother dropped a tray of snacks she had prepared for their arrival.

Lucy rushed to her mother's aid while apologizing profusely. "Lucy! Be quiet, I'm fine. Now go to your father as he appears ready to have a heart attack."

After everyone was settled Lucy introduced the other arrivals and informed her parents that she had mated with David Pearson, who she loved with all her heart. Margo Tomasi asked, "Lucy, tell me the relationships these others have with you?"

"Oh! I'm sorry Mother. Laura Pearson is the twin of David who mated with James Blake at the same time as David and I."

Margo glanced at her husband, Hitoshi Tomasi. "Not in the same room I hope!"

By this time Lucy was so embarrassed and flustered that Laura interrupted. "David and I are the children of Aaron and Alice Pearson, agents for the High Priestess. We are also undercover agents and because we don't interact with other Blues, the angel Barbara sought mates for us. At our first separate meeting we mated. I'll let Lucy tell you how that came about, but for now we want to make arrangements for the bonding ceremony. Margo does your family have a wedding dress?"

"Your parents are the world-wide heroes Aaron and Alice Pearson! They have awesome psi powers, and Lucy you're now part of that family! Oh, what honor you bring to our family. Wait a moment, you teleported here. That's something only the Pearson's could do, so your mating with David must have given you that ability."

"Yes, Mother and so much more. Your little girl is going to be an agent too, but let's talk about a wedding dress, does the family have one?"

Margo ran to her husband and they hugged as she cried into

his shoulder. "Mom! What's wrong?"

Margo regained control of her emotions as she took Lucy's hand and left the room. Ten minutes later they returned with Lucy carrying a large box, which she placed on the floor. The women carefully unwrapped the dress inside the box until Margo held it up. It appeared to be quite old and was white, covered in lace and had a short train in the back.

"Oh Mom! This is beautiful. Was it yours?"

Margo nodded her head. Yes, it's been in our family a very long time, over 200 years. It's much longer than the newer gowns, but we must see what adjustments we need to make, so let's try it on.

When the women left the room, Hitoshi said, "Gentlemen, while we have some time would you join me in a toast to your mating. At their quick smiles he quickly went to a cabinet where he poured three glasses of sa'ki, which he heated before handing them to his guests. Holding up his glass he said, "To a long and fruitful marriage."

The men were interrupted in their conversation when the women returned with Lucy wearing the wedding dress. David and James had never seen such a dress before. It had a full skirt that dragged the floor and a train that followed her, as she seemed to float across the floor. The dress was covered in lace and had a veil that hung like gauze from a small hat. The bodice was low, but modestly covered her breasts. Margo triumphantly said, "It fits perfectly after I took in the bodice a little. Lucy is a little taller than me which makes the length perfect for her."

Laura said, "Okay, let's get it back into the box and discuss where the ceremony is to be held."

Once everyone was back into the living area, Margo passed around the salvaged snacks and drinks. Laura cleared her throat getting everyone's attention. "Margo, if we have this ceremony in the States how many guests will you bring. I'm saying this because the High Priestess is going to be involved somehow, either in person or by vid."

Margo looked at her husband in surprise before shaking her head in disappointment. "Tokyo is too crowded and having the venue here would be too expensive and crowded, even if held in the Temple. We would bring six close relatives and friends for a total of eight."

They continued the discussion about notification and where to meet to be teleported to the venue, not yet determined. Eventually, Lucy and members of her new family said their goodbyes and they teleported to James Blake's home in Greater LA Metro of Southern California. James had learned his lesson from Lucy and mentally informed his parents that they would arrive by teleportation.

Peter and Mary Blake were in the kitchen when the group arrived in the living room. James called, "Mother, Dad where are you?"

Mary raised her voice, "We're in here. Take a seat and we'll be right out."

James' parents soon appeared bringing snacks and drinks that they set on a table. "Mom, Dad I want you to meet my mate, Laura Pearson and her twin, David with his mate Lucy Tomasi. Everyone, these are my parents, Peter and Mary Blake."

His parents looked at them with surprise for a moment before Mary replied, "You're not joking, are you?"

"No Mom, you've heard the news about the reappearance of the angel Barbara in conjunction with the Temple's Agents Aaron and Alice Pearson. Well, Laura and David are the children of Aaron and Alice and the angel Barbara picked Lucy and myself to be their mates."

Peter blurted, "You've got to be kidding us. I didn't put much credence in the news of the angel Barbara sighting. But this, it's just too much!"

Suddenly, Barbara appeared which caused Peter to stumble backwards and fall to the floor. He quickly regained his feet and gave her a deep bow. "I'm deeply sorry your grace for my disbelief. Your absence has been too long. What can I do to gain your forgiveness?"

"Look at me! Can you not feel my love? These young people have been given a task by God to show his people that he is still watching over them. Hear them out and give them all your love and support."

Barbara turned to the mated pairs and smiled. "Again I did well with this selection. Pick a large venue as the High Priestess will be in attendance."

Her loving smile was so intense that it brought tears of

happiness to all those in the room. Then she disappeared.

Laura muttered, "Crap! This means were going to need somewhere large enough to hold several thousand people. That probably means a large domed arena. Anybody have a better idea?"

David thought a moment before saying, "I'll ask Natalie if she has an idea."

All the young people eavesdropped on the David's mental conversation and when finished they each had smiles on their faces. Laura said, "Well done David. If Natalie follows through with her idea we'll have the venue in Kansas City at the Harry S. Truman Coliseum. She'll get back to us on the near future dates that will be available."

Mary and Peter looked confused for a moment, and then Mary said, "So the mating ceremony for both of you is going to be in Kansas City. That's not going to take us long to get there by bullet train or shuttle. Are you going to have a reception?"

Laura grimaced. "Yes, but that's still not settled. Once we determine how many people are going to be interested in the reception, then we'll seek a place to hold it. It's probably going to be a catered affair."

David said, "Laura and I live in Kansas City along with our parents, so we have a handle on what's available. At this point we have to wait until we know how many people are going to attend. I don't think we can financially handle the whole arena, even if all the parents chip in."

"David, let's not panic. Barbara wouldn't let us hang on finances. We'll ask Natalie about that when she gives us the available dates for the coliseum. Peter, how many people from here do you think will come for our ceremony?"

Peter and Mary went to the kitchen table and started compiling a list, while the others researched the size of the coliseum and what features it offered. They were eating take-out when Natalie contacted them about the availability of the coliseum. The first available date was Thursday of next week, and then it was another thirty-eight days before an open date.

The twins and their mates quickly decided on the first date and asked Natalie to book it. Laura then broached the subject of payment. "Natalie who's paying for this?"

There was no response for several seconds and the silence was becoming unbearable until Natalie chuckled. "The Temple of course. You wouldn't be in this fix if the High Priestess wasn't attending. The cost of the reception is on us as well. Go ahead and make the arrangements and have them bill us. If I were you I'd have the best Bar-b-que restaurants cater the event. Contact at the coliseum is Dot Paterson, so talk to her about your arrangements."

Three hours later they were back in Kansas City in the twins' old apartment. Laura immediately called Dot Paterson, the coliseum's event manager, and made an appointment for the following morning. The twins and their mates made separate piles of their belongings that they then teleported to their new apartments. Tomorrow James and Lucy would shop for new clothing to last until they could retrieve their own.

The next day they all met for breakfast at one of the nearby restaurants. Then Laura went to the coliseum and David guided the others on their shopping trip. Laura consulted with Dot Paterson about having the reception at the venue and they arrived at a plan. They would have three serving lines in the outside hallways at the midlevel part of the coliseum and if the various restaurant staff were agreeable, each line would serve a variety from each restaurant.

Laura then started calling the top Bar-b-que restaurants in Kansas City to make the arrangements. Eventually, she used the event to foster competition between the four best restaurants, as each would offer what they were best noted for, whether it was ribs, brisket, pulled pork, etc.

Serving size was to be small so the patrons could sample each offering. At the serving line each offering would be labeled as to the providing restaurant and the patrons would vote for whom they considered the best. The winning restaurant would receive a 10,000-credit award and a vid announcement of the winner.

When Laura notified the restaurants' management of the contest, they started cutting their fees each vying to be one of those selected. When everything was arranged Laura smiled to herself, her little contest ploy had saved enough ten times over to pay the 10,000-credit award.

Laura mentally contacted her mother and asked if they were at home before teleporting there. Aaron and Alice greeted their daughter by each giving her a kiss and hug. Alice drew her over the couch. "Well, how's it going? Tell us what you've arranged."

Laura related her experiences in Tokyo and the Greater LA Metro, including the visit from Barbara. Then the High Priestesses planned attendance causing the selection of Kansas City and the Harry S. Truman Coliseum as the site of the venue.

Alice looked at her daughter in awe. "You and the others did all that! Honey, you should get a medal for how you put all that together. So, eleven a.m., Thursday of next week. I can't quite get my head around my babies going to their mating ceremony."

"Oh, Mom. Wait until your grandchildren start all this again. It's like Angel is emerging again turning the world upside down. Now! Are we having flowers?"

CHAPTER EIGHTEEN

It was the day of the mating ceremony. Laura and Lucy were in Aaron and Alice's apartment donning their wedding dresses with the help of both their mothers. Alice and Margo looked at their daughters with tears in their eyes until Margo took a big breath.

"They both look like angels in those dresses. Have you ever seen such beautiful women before, even if I'm a little prejudiced?"

Alice dabbed at her eyes with a finger before getting a tissue and blowing her nose. "No, you're absolutely correct and I'm thinking no one has ever seen such beautiful wedding dresses together like this in over a hundred years."

Lucy chuckled. "David just heard that people have been filing into the coliseum for over an hour and we have almost three hours left before it starts. Laura I hope we ordered enough food for the reception."

"The vendors said they were preparing enough food for 25,000 people. I can't think of any reason why we should have more than half that number, but God works in strange ways."

The twins, their mates and immediate family all teleported to the fifty-yard line where a stage had been erected. A hush fell over the Coliseum when they appeared. The High Priestess was already present and when the twins and their mates started climbing the steps to the stage a wedding march began playing.

The two brides and their mates were highlighted on large vid monitors causing the women in the audience to loudly inhale in awe. The crowd almost filled the lower tier of the coliseum that held 28,000 seats. It was well they had selected such a large venue. When the two mating parties stood before the Priestess, their immediate family took their places five paces behind them.

The High Priestess started by giving everyone a short history of the Pearson family beginning with Angel Pearson, the Healing Guild's first healer and the evolution has continued until now where they had healing Temples throughout the world.

"We have before us direct descendants of Angel Pearson who are mating with members of the Healing Guild that were selected by the angel Barbara. Yes, the angel Barbara has returned and she has brought the word of God! The Pearson's have been selected to again make His presence known through their efforts to help mankind. You already know what Aaron and Laura Pearson have achieved, now we have four more. I want you to witness their mating ceremony today and remember this historic occasion. Now let the ceremony begin!"

Thirty minutes later the ceremony was completed and the couples stood at two receiving lines in an effort to speed up the proceedings. Some of the guests elected to eat first knowing how long this was going to take. Three hours later the mated couples and their immediate families were eating with the High Priestess and Natalie in one of the private rooms of the coliseum.

The Priestess held up a rib she had just finished. "Laura I'm glad you took my suggestion about serving Bar-b-que. This is excellent food. Now that we have three pairs of agents we have greater flexibility in how assignments are conducted. Initially, Aaron and Alice will select assignments until everyone is seasoned. Laura didn't you foresee that problem in India?"

"Yes and no. I knew we would achieve our goals without any losses, but not that I would be shot in the butt. However, my armor mostly worked. David healed the bruise."

Alice interrupted. "You got shot? Laura you know my instructions about entering a room you know has multi-assailants."

Laura and David said together, "You freeze everyone with a weapon!"

"I bet I know what happened here, you were afraid for the

hostages so you went in fast and you got shot. What if a hostage had been shot instead, would you still call it a win?"

Laura hung her head. "No, I've learned my lesson. That's one situation I won't repeat."

The Priestess slowly smiled at her charges. "See, everyone learns from this hiccup and hopefully it won't be repeated."

She turned to the other parents. "This has been the first time any of the agents have been injured and if they abide by their training it should be the last. I want agents to be proficient in at least one other language other than their birth language. Before you start make sure one of the other agents isn't already knowledgeable in it. That way you can function better in a foreign country."

Mary Blake asked, "James, do both you and Lucy have the same powers as your mates?"

"Yes, but we aren't yet proficient in their use. I expect we will be soon as we gain more experience. Don't worry Mom, we are well protected."

Natalie spoke up, "In case you're interested, you had 26,389 guests at your ceremony and the small amount of food leftovers was taken to the Temple. I believe we have set several new records at this mating ceremony. Most attended, best food according to the reviews, first presided over by a High Priestess, and first with two couples."

Aaron chuckled. "Yeah, I bet this one won't be forgotten for those reasons and how beautiful the brides were in their dresses."

* * *

Two weeks later the two new teams were back in Kansas City after an extended honeymoon where each newly mated pair learned much about each other and now were eager to learn their new jobs. The group teleported from Aaron and Alice's apartment to a mountain ridge overlooking a peaceful meadow.

Aaron explained how they selected their assignments, which brought immediate questions from the new recruits. James asked, "Who prepares these files?"

Aaron and Alice looked at each other for a moment and then smiled. Alice replied, "We have asked ourselves the same thing.

We finally deduced that this was God's work. While mind merged we found this site already prepared for us. Whether it was God or his angels doesn't matter. The stinky level determines the time sensitivity and degree of threat. The greatest threat we have encountered to date was when we encountered the nuclear bomb threat in Scotland. The stink level was so great we both had to fight our gag reflex."

Lucy's face had turned white when she blurted, "But obviously you were able to work through it."

"Yes, but when we found the bomb we didn't know it was nuclear, just that the timer was about to expire so we tossed it as high upwards as we could. In the future teleport bombs into the Sun."

Aaron looked at the two eager newbie's. "Alright, Alice and I are going to mind merge while you tag along. We will pick the worst smelling, tasting file available and open it. Don't gag!'

Aaron and Alice mind merged and started their short journey to their destination. As they drew near the site their senses were bombarded with a disgusting smell and taste. They removed the file that was obviously the worst by how disgusting it appeared. They opened the file, reviewed its contents and withdrew back to the ridge.

James and Lucy were both struggling to retain their breakfast, while the others were paler than usual. After a few minutes Alice asked the newbie's, "Are you both okay?"

At their nod, she asked, "What should we do, if anything?"

Lucy grimaced before answering. "This is actionable because otherwise it wouldn't be in the file. I thought the slave trade had been eliminated. This is disgusting and we have to take action even if it involves people within a country's government!"

Aaron nodded his head in agreement. "Yes, but whom do we turn them over to prosecute?"

James frowned. "Maybe the World Court?"

"Very good. But before we take this type of action that will bring worldwide notice, we must first notify Control. The High Priestess will have to give her approval, as this will affect the local Temple. Follow my mental conversation with Natalie."

Control, this is Aaron.

Yes Aaron, what's the problem?

We have pulled a stinky file that involves slave trading in the small desert country of Quater. Does this require the Priestess's approval?

Wait until I check!

Okay, you're good. Teleport the offenders to our previously approved detention area. The World Court will retrieve them. Good luck.

Aaron looked at the others. "You heard, so we're good to go. Let's teleport back to my apartment so we can research where we're going."

Later, after doing their research they decided to wait six hours because of the time difference before teleporting to Quater's seat of government. Each couple agreed to try to rest and eat before returning at the appointed time.

When they returned to their leaders apartment they teleported to Quater's main government building, which was next to the Palace where the President resided. They immediately placed a protective shield around their small group before they entered the building. Their plan was to spread out like a fan for the first four agents, followed by the remaining two whose job was to protect their rear and teleport those frozen by the lead agents who had deemed them slavers by mind scans.

They were in the building fifteen minutes before internal security made their presence known. At first it was one uniformed officer who was quickly frozen in place, then quickly it multiplied as more and more men arrived, then as quickly they withdrew as the agents froze the leaders in place. The agents followed about ten men until they stopped before two large doors they were attempting to guard.

The uniformed men were frozen in place and then moved to one side as the agents forced the doors open. They found over fifty men inside who were looking at them in surprise and fear. Lucy and David stood as the rear guard as the other four advanced into the room. Aaron shouted, "Anyone here speak English?"

When there was no response, Alice mentally pulled a man out of the group until he stood quivering before her. "You understand English! Tell the others we want only those who deal in slavery. If you know of any, point them out and we will leave the others alone."

After the man repeated Alice's announcement, nothing happened except fearful looks among the captives. Then one by one people started rising above the others and were moved to a separate group where they were frozen. As this group became larger several men panicked and tried to break away and leave the room; however, they soon joined the frozen group.

Ten minutes later the frozen group contained twenty-one men. The others regarded the frozen group with contempt. The man Alice had picked who understood English said, "My name is Anwar Alabdulathem. You did well, but you missed several that were not here."

"Were they somewhere between here and the front of the building?"

"Yes. You should also consider the President and his staff. They are as guilty as those you have selected."

"What will your country do with so many of its top members absent?"

"Flourish, with those swine not feeding from the trough."

"Do you know who we are?"

He smiled at her. "Of course, you are one of the Pearson's. Your group has grown. I have never seen such wondrous things before. Are you going to free the slaves?"

"Yes. Would you gather them so we can make arrangements for them?"

"It would be my honor. Would one week from today meet your requirements?"

"Yes. How many slaves do you estimate?"

"10,000 at least. Many were born here. If they desire to remain here as free citizens would that be allowed?"

"Yes, if they truly desire to remain here."

"Very well, it has been an honor to know you. Be wary of the President's security."

When the entire slaver group was teleported they turned their attention to the President and his staff. First they mind scanned those present next door in the Presidential Palace to determine what their security plans were before making their own assault plans.

The agent's teleported to the front doors of the Palace while maintaining their protective shields. They then used their powers to remove the doors into the Palace, before walking inside through a hail of projectile and laser fire. They then froze everyone inside the building causing a sudden silence to fall over the battlefield.

Aaron pointed to each agent to begin their assigned tasks while he and Alice continued inside walking to where the President had hid himself. They forced their way into the old throne room, now the Presidential Office where the President was frozen under his desk. Alice used her powers to move him to the center of the room before helping Aaron move six others to join the President. These turned out to be his official staff and were complacent with the President in the slave trade.

Aaron teleported the slaver group to the assigned pickup point before checking with the other agents. They reported no other guilty parties, so they released everyone else from their frozen condition before teleporting back to their starting point in Kansas City.

CHAPTER NINETEEN

The agents reported to Natalie the following day. Natalie examined the faces of the newbie's before asking, "James, Lucy do you have any thoughts or questions about this assignment?"

Lucy frowned in confusion. "From my analysis of the slavers' thoughts this slave business has been going on for decades. Why wasn't it stopped before this?"

"Do you mean us or the world leaders? Apparently it was well hidden until you opened the stinky file. By the way, I don't like that term. It brings to mind a really bad situation...I guess I answered my own question."

Laura retrieved from her memory the slaver stinky file and mentally showed it to Natalie. She looked at Laura in surprise before her face showed disgust, revulsion, and finally green with sickness as she quickly grabbed a container to throw-up into.

Lucy quickly brought her a wet towel to clean up. Natalie eventually took a deep breath and her color returned to normal. She glared at Laura for a moment, then quirked her mouth in acceptance. "That was the only way for me to truly know what you have to endure when you go after a *stinky file*. If anything you understated it! That's horrible!"

Alice nodded her head. "After the first dozen times you learn to blunt the effects. Lucy and James handled it quite well for their first time. In Quater we met a lawmaker who was helpful once he was assured that we were going to remove all the slavers. His name is Anwar Alabdulathem and has agreed to gather all the slaves for us a week from yesterday. He estimated that there were about 10,000 slaves and some may want to stay if they have full freedoms. We need to make preparations for their disposition."

Natalie contemplated this news for a moment before holding up her finger for them to wait while she mentally contacted the Priestess. Shortly thereafter she smiled. "The Priestess wishes to thank you personally, so if you will follow me."

When the agents arrived in the Priestess's private quarters they greeted her with a short bow. She in turn approached each agent and gave them a kiss on the forehead, then stepped back and smiled through her tears of happiness. "Freeing those slaves is one of my fondest achievements and you did it without any loss of life. In addition, your actions may have resulted in a country achieving true freedom. I have already asked the World Court to take responsibility for any slaves who wish to relocate. I am sure that the vid networks will soon demand an interview, so return home in your Blues and prepare yourselves."

Before the agents left the Temple, Aaron said, "Meet in our apartment in an hour looking your best. You all did well today and Alice and I are very proud of you."

* * *

A year later the three teams of agents had gained worldwide attention and acclaim for they're many actions. Three countries had given them medals for their life saving efforts. The High Priestess had replicas made of all their awards and medals and put them on display in the lobby of each Temple worldwide. The High Priestess wanted everyone to view her agents' accomplishments.

When the award display was opened at the Kansas City World Headquarters of The Healing Guild, the vid networks were on hand to make sure everyone knew their accomplishments. The agents were dressed in special Blues that had thin red piping around the shoulder seams and a wide red stripe on each sleeve cuff. They each proudly wore their medals for everyone to admire.

Anwar Alabdulathem, the new President of Quater was on

hand to present each of them medals for freeing the slaves and the people of Quater from its repressive government. After the ceremony the new President personally thanked each team member and then motioned to a young woman dressed in her country's customary wear. "This is Alice Alabdulathem, one of the freed slaves. She took Agent Alice Pearson's first name and my last name to honor those who helped free her. She was a house slave and received a good education including English language skills. She agreed to be my assistant and expressed an interest in meeting all of you."

Alice Pearson smiled at the young woman. "I'm honored that you took part of my name. How old are you?"

The young Alice blushed and bowed deeply to her. "I'm twenty-three and the one honored to at last meet my namesake as one of those responsible for freeing me. Since gaining my freedom I'm now aware of the many things you and your family have done for the world. If you need anything from me you have only to ask."

Alice Pearson's eyes teared up and she gave the young Alice a hug before releasing her. Before turning away they both had tears in their eyes.

Later that night while snuggling close to Aaron, Alice related her experience with the former slave Alice. He turned to face his mate. "Babe, it's not often we connect with people outside the Temple. If you like you can mentally contact her from time to time to see how she is doing. I think it would do you both good."

Alice hugged her mate tightly as she resolved to do just that. Tomorrow the team would select three assignments from the stinky files. The young ones were now experienced enough to fully support their teams. She thought Lucy was going to be as strong a personality as Laura and wondered if Barbara's selection used that as a strong indicator.

The next day Aaron pulled three stinky files and without looking inside passed Laura and David each a file. "Look inside, consult with your mate and in fifteen minutes or less give us a recap of the problems and solution."

Alice looked at their file and then passed it to Aaron. Ten minutes later, the other two teams approached them. Alice asked, "Who wants to go first?"

David nodded to Laura who began. "Ours is a simple robbery

and extortion attempt. Someone is going to try to steal our medals from the London Temple and hold them for ransom. I doubt they would succeed, but we will be there to prevent injuries."

At Alice's nod David began. "Someone is thinking that kidnapping a Red and forcing her to perform her services for a fee is a risk-free way of making a lot of credits. This threat is against the Paris Temple and we plan on monitoring thoughts until finding the person responsible."

Alice held up their file. "Ours is a problem on the Mars Colony. Anyone want to switch?"

Laura asked, "Can you wait until our assignments are finished? I would really like to monitor your assignment."

"We have a time sensitive assignment, but you can review our memories later. Go ahead and start your assignments and if you need help contact us."

After the other teams left Alice grimaced. "We might have to call them in to help us."

"Let's get some more information first. Let's try Lt. Colonel Jennifer Meyers first. She was our first military contact and later when we were teleporting supplies to the Mars Colony." Aaron mentally searched for her until he connected, whereupon he asked for a meet. Aaron and Alice then immediately teleported to her office in Houston. She had aged well over the years and from the ring on her hand she was married. She smiled at them when they appeared and came around her desk to shake their hands and gave them a rueful smile.

"You two usually bring unwelcome news when it's an unscheduled visit, what's up?"

Aaron asked, "When was your last contact with Mars?"

Meyers' face turned pale as she touched her implant. "Jill find out when we had our last contact with the Colony and what was discussed."

A few minutes later her finger touched her jaw as she received a reply and her eyes unconsciously met theirs, then she gave them a smile as she said, "Thanks Jill, I'll get back with you."

Meyers raised her eyebrow at the agents. "Routine conversation twelve hours ago, no problems. What's your concern?"

Alice shrugged her shoulders. "We've got some nonspecific

indication that the Colony was in immediate danger. How many domes do they have and how spread out are they?"

Meyers looked at them for a moment. "Follow me and I'll show you something that might help."

The agents followed her into an office two doors down that contained a large-scale model of the Mars Colony. It showed one large dome surrounded by four smaller domes in a starburst pattern. Aaron asked, "How large an area does the domes cover?"

"About 650 meters circumference, why?"

Alice replied, "We were considering placing a force field over the area. What are the Colony's greatest threats?"

"Wait a moment, I want someone more knowledgeable to answer that question."

She then used her implant to summon someone. A younger woman in civilian clothing soon joined them. Meyers said, "Julie Sherian, these are the famous Aaron and Alice Pearson you have been hearing about. Tell them what the greatest threats are to the Colony."

Julie quickly rushed forward and shook their hands, then considered their question. "You must suspect a quick disaster, not a lingering problem. Number one would be a meteor strike, followed by a storm. Meteor is more likely because they can see a storm approaching. Even this is unlikely, maybe one chance in 10,000 it would hit the Colony - 100,000 or more for one big enough to destroy it."

"Okay, would you get us a picture of a large area inside the big dome?" Aaron said before shrugging his shoulders. "I can't think of anything else we can do."

Alice contemplated for a few seconds. "Let's have the others us meet here and get their input!"

A few minutes later the others arrived and were looking at the model while receiving a brief of the problem. Laura shook her head in disbelief. "So you think going there and setting up a force field is the best bet? How big a rock do you think it's going to be?"

Aaron thought a moment then pointed at Julie, who said, "Probably about the size of a robo cab, but weighing over 100 times more."

Laura responded, "Wow! That's going to be a big bang. Wouldn't it be better to push it back into space?"

Aaron and Alice mentally consulted with the other teams about who were the most powerful members with telekinesis, the ability to move objects with their minds. The final consensus was that the best course would be to use all members working together. After arriving on Mars they would first establish a protective force field, then they would stand outside to watch for the meteor's arrival. Together they might be able to divert its path away from the Colony, hopefully back into space.

Aaron asked Meyers, "We will need environmental suits. Do you have any here or can we use spares from the Colony?"

Meyers frowned. "They may not have your size. Read my memories, I'm picturing where we need to go. The team members helped teleport Sherian and Meyers to a warehouse fifty kilometers away. Lt. Colonel Meyers ordered the supervisor to provide the team members with environment suits that had extra oxygen capacity. They might have to stay outside for a long period of time.

Everyone took a bathroom break before donning the suits and teleporting to the Colony. They arrived outside the main dome and immediately raised the force shield over the Colony. The team then walked to an area where they had the best view of the sky and started their watch for the meteor. As chance would have it they were looking at a night sky that looked different from what they were used to seeing.

They were advised to concentrate their watch on the northeast sky, but with all the people they had they covered every direction. Lucy mused to herself, *this the most beautiful sight I've ever experienced.*

After looking at the sky for almost an hour, their eyes started to wander around looking at their surroundings, noting how quiet it was. Laura spotted the bright object first that began to move toward them. They all concentrated their efforts to move the meteor's trajectory upwards in an effort to make it skip off Mars' thin atmosphere and back into space. After five minutes they knew they had failed, but the trajectory had changed enough that the meteor streaked over their heads by at least fifteen kilometers, a ball of fire roaring loudly that turned night to day.

The Colony was located inside a large crater and the meteor soon passed over the rim that from their prospective appeared to be low hills. Ten seconds later there was a bright flash that gave the appearance of a sunrise that soon dissipated and was night again. Suddenly, the ground gave a sharp shift then a sway before returning to a stable condition. When the shock wave arrived from the explosion, it was minor because of the thin atmosphere and distance from the impact.

Unexpectedly, about three minutes later the force field started to repeal debris from the impact that continued for several minutes. While they waited for the fallout to end, three people from the Colony joined them. One of the colonists who was distinguished from the others by red stripes around his arms, spoke, "Who are you people and what just happened?"

Aaron replied, "My name is Aaron Pearson, my mate Alice, our children Laura and David, and their mates James and Lucy. We teleported here in an effort to try to save the colony from a meteor strike, which apparently we did. As soon as the debris stops falling we'll remove the force field and leave. You may contact Earth and tell them we were successful in our efforts. The meteor hit outside the rim about forty-eight kilometers southwest of here, it might have uncovered something interesting for you to study."

There was a loud thud as something large impacted the force field, then slid off. It glowed as everyone watched it in fascination. "Dr. Graham, we must check that out immediately!" Said one of the other colonists.

Aaron looked at his group and smiled. "Our work here is finished."

He removed the force field and they teleported back to where they had departed and returned their Mars suits. The other two teams then returned to where they were before helping with this assignment, while Aaron and Alice returned to Lt. Colonel Meyers' office. She gave a little start when they appeared, but then smiled. "You made it back okay! What happened?"

Laura said, "We couldn't move it back into space, but were able to divert it away from the Colony. As a side note, a big piece of something fell next to the station that is being investigated by your people. If you need us you know how we can be reached."

.

CHAPTER TWENTY

When Aaron and Alice returned to their apartment they sat together drinking coffee trying to relax. Before reviewing the actions of their children's teams on the Mars assignment, Laura mused, "Have you considered why that meteor waited until we were in place to take care of it?"

"You think God was watching over us?"

"That, or He was pulling the strings for this whole emergency."

Aaron considered his mate's theory and then nodded his head. "You might be right, but that's probably true of everything we do. He gives us a push and watches what we do. The kids did pretty good, didn't they?"

"Yeah, I really liked Laura's idea to try pushing it back into space even though all we managed was to move it away from the Colony site."

"We learned what our joint capabilities were if we ever have to do something like that again."

"Yeah, it was like trying to grab a slippery fish out of the water."

Aaron chuckled, "Hey, that's a good analogy. Next time we should push up rather than trying to grab it."

"Let's wait on the others to return before reporting to Control.

Its past time for lunch, are you hungry?"

Later, when the other two teams returned from their assignments they teleported to Control. After changing into their Blues they entered Natalie's office. She nodded her head at them then sat back in her chair observing them. "I just received a surprise call from the President praising your actions on Mars. What was that about?"

Alice ruefully smiled. "We opened another stinky file that warned of problems at the Mars Colony. When Aaron and I investigated we were convinced that a meteor strike was imminent, so we called in the other teams for help and we got there in time to divert it elsewhere. The other teams then returned to their assignments."

Natalie frowned at her. "I believe that story was barely an outline of what really happened. Laura please expand a little more!"

She looked at her mother and shook her head. "Natalie, you know her well. She is shy about describing herself as a hero. This is the first time any of us has teleported to another planet and we weren't sure about the meteor strike being the problem. We all wore environment suits for the first time and thankfully had no problems with them. Otherwise, I had a great time experiencing Mars at night. When the meteor arrived we tried to shove it back into space, but were only able to divert it away from the colony. The force field we had established protected the colony from falling debris after the meteor struck Mars. No one was harmed, so I count it as a win for us."

Natalie's face had turned pale during the description of their Mars odyssey. When Laura finished with her tale, Natalie blurted, "You could have been killed! All of you!"

Aaron interrupted, "Alice and I have a theory about the stinky files. We believe they are prepared by God's angels and as such have His protection when we act upon them. That's why I brought the whole team together for this assignment."

Natalie closed her eyes and said a silent prayer of thanksgiving for their successful completion of this dangerous mission. She then asked David and Laura about their assignments. When finished, Natalie complimented them all.

"President Harper wants you all to come to the White House

for a dinner next Tuesday. I think he wants to surprise you with another medal, so be surprised if it happens. However, he may also want you to do something for him. He was keeping his thoughts hidden behind a leaking mind shield. I'll be there too, so wear your Dress Blues. Meet here at six p.m. and we'll teleport together."

* * *

They arrived at the White House portico as instructed where the President's Chief of Staff, Wanda Davenport, met them. She greeted everyone warmly and asked everyone to follow her. Two armed immaculately dressed Marines trailed them as they followed Davenport and three SS agents to the family quarters where they lost their armed escort.

Davenport, an attractive brunette, had a reputation of being a no-nonsense individual who aggressively protected her boss, stopped before a room with double doors. "The President and First Lady would like you to join them for refreshments before dinner. Please follow me and I will introduce you."

They followed her inside and discovered they were the only guests. After introductions they broke into two groups by gender. Davenport circled between the groups ensuring that no one was slighted, and then the President and First Lady switched groups. Later, as they were shown into the Dining Room they realized each of the Presidential pair was skilled in judging people.

After dinner, while enjoying a fine wine, President Harper asked, "Since you all were on Mars for several hours would you give me your impressions? Let's start with Laura."

"Initially, I was concentrating on spotting the meteor. But after a while I became aware of the stark landscape illuminated by two moons and the stars. Due to the thin atmosphere the stars were bright and crisp and I wondered if one of the more brilliant ones was Earth. Next was the silence. I could hear myself breathing. That all changed when the meteor passed overhead. It sounded like a living thing as it roared over our heads."

Jessica Harper, the First Lady, sat with her mouth open as Laura described her experience, then exclaimed, "My! I wish I could have seen that. Did you all have that same thrill?"

Lucy grimaced. "I did until it grumbled and growled overhead like a living thing. Then later when the fallout from the explosion started falling onto the force field I was startled when a chunk of the meteor hit the shield and slid to the ground glowing malevolently. It still gives me the shivers."

President Harper shook himself out of his mental visualization her description gave him. "I have a favor I would like you to do for us. That chunk of rock is too radioactive for anyone to get near it, as they have no equipment to deal with something like that. We want you to take a shielded container there, use your powers to place it into the box and bring it back to Earth."

Natalie asked, "How sure are you that the shielded box is adequate to the task?"

"The equipment on Mars indicated that the box is sufficiently shielded. We have a facility that has safeguards for something like this."

Aaron asked, "When do you want it?"

"ASAP. How about tomorrow one of you teleport to the location of this picture, pick up the box and after collecting the object on Mars, return to the same location."

Aaron and Alice looked at Natalie with raised eyebrows who nodded her head in acceptance. Aaron smiled slightly. "Okay, we agree to take on this little task, but you better take extra safeguards with this piece of rock. We all have misgivings about it. I would rather toss it back into space or better yet into the Sun."

President Harper contemplated Aaron's words carefully before saying; "If I have second thoughts I'll contact you before you leave Earth. Now let's get to the awarding of the Special Medal I made up for you for saving the Mars Colony."

Everyone left the dinner table and followed him to another room where six gleaming medals lay on a table along with an engraved plaque. President Harper picked up one of the medals, holding it so they could all see. "It's called the *Pearson Medal*, and its first presentation is to the descendants of Angel Pearson. The award is for selfless heroism in the face of great personal risk of life to save the people of the Mars Colony. The plaque details what you did and I want to give this to the person who returns to Mars to hang in the proper place of honor. Now, when I call your name step forward and receive your medal."

After the medals were given out the President smiled at the

group and said, "Well done. This medal business is not so much a pat on the back, but a way to show the world what you've done. To show everyone we must all step up when we can make a difference. I'm sure you will show up here again, but maybe not before me personally, to receive an award for something heroic you've done. I wish you well and it's been a privilege to know you."

* * *

A year later the agents were called to the Kansas City Temple for a meeting with the Priestess. Natalie led the way to a conference room where she asked everyone to take a seat until the Priestess could join them. After fifteen minutes they began to get restless as none of them were used to inactivity.

Five minutes later the Priestess entered closely followed by two people dressed in civilian clothes. The agents rose as she entered the room and walked to the head of the table where she looked uneasily at her people. She turned to the man and woman who were standing near her. "This is Herman Goseling and Sheila Schmutz, Security Agents from the European Union. They have a problem they want your help with. President Harper and I have endorsed their request if you decide to help. Herman, Sheila I'll leave it to you explain your request."

Sheila replaced the Priestess who had left the room. "Who is your spokesperson?"

Natalie raised her hand. "That would be me. What is your problem that only we can solve?"

Sheila raised her eyebrow at that response. "A little testy are we? Our problem is also yours. There is a faction within the Union that is targeting religious organizations. In the last six months sixteen churches of various denominations have been firebombed, so far with no loss of life. Your temples have not yet been targeted, maybe because of your group's reputation. The High Priestess assures us that the Healing Guild has had no part in the firebombing and has pledged your help in stopping it."

Natalie frowned in thought. "Maybe this faction is only targeting houses of worship, we only heal illnesses. Although, we do stress that this healing is from God. What would you have us do?"

Sheila slowly smiled. "We want you to use your special powers to root out these people and turn them over to us for prosecution."

Natalie turned to Aaron. "How many of your team do you need for this?"

He mentally consulted with Alice before answering, "Just Laura and James for now. If they need help we can add more people."

Natalie addressed Sheila; "You've got our support, where do you want us to start?"

"We've noted a pattern, so I would recommend they start in Cologne, Germany."

Laura and James mentally conferred, then walked up to the Union Agents and introduced themselves. Laura then asked, "Do you have luggage or have any other things to do here? We have no authority in Germany or the Union, so you need to directly work with us."

They looked at her in surprise, but then Sheila said, "Our luggage is at the reception desk and our flight to Europe leaves this afternoon."

"Very well, follow us as we need to change into civilian clothing before leaving." Laura and James led the other Agents to the reception area where they retrieved their luggage then led them to Natalie's office where they had the European Union Agents wait while they changed clothing.

Coming out of the change room Laura asked, "Have either of you been to Cologne before?"

Sheila answered with a little squeak in her voice, "Yes, we both have."

"Good! Sheila, picture a landmark that you know well so that we can anchor onto it. Yes, that will do nicely. Grab your luggage and away we go!"

Sheila and Herman, both looking a little confused realized that they were now in Cologne standing before a large Catholic Church. Sheila breathed a sigh of relief. "That's better than a three hour shuttle ride! Wow, when I realized what you were getting us ready for I about froze up. What now?"

"Let's get rid of your luggage. Call a robo cab and have it

delivered to a hotel of your choice while we get a lay of the land."

They soon found themselves seated at an outdoor café drinking an espresso and eating a pastry. Laura licked her fingers. "Yummy that tasted good. Did you like yours Jimmy?"

"Kansas City doesn't have anything like this. Should we get another?"

"We better not, these two are giving us the stink eye so we better get to work. Okay we'll let our minds wander and see if we get a nibble."

The European Agents watched the Temple agents, as they seemed to go into a trance for several minutes until they both blinked their eyes and smiled. Laura and James smiled at each other and bumped their fists together before Laura said, "That church we arrived at is going to be a target early tomorrow morning. I felt three minds, but there may be more involved. What do you want to do?"

Sheila grimaced. "The only people I can muster this soon is the local police and I can't trust that some of them might be involved. Can you get some of your people to help here?"

"Our closest Temple is Berlin. Have either of you been there?"

Sheila grinned. "I'll do you one better. I've been to the Temple."

CHAPTER TWENTY-ONE

The four were soon standing before the Berlin Temple with everyone following Laura inside. She requested the receptionist summon the Chief of Security. It wasn't long before they were standing before his desk. Laura identified herself and James as agents for the Priestess and the other two as agents for the European Union and their reason for being here.

COS John Boeckstiegel asked, "What can I do for you?"

Laura asked, "Does your staff have the ability to freeze in place individuals?"

He gave a lopsided grin. "We don't have your powers, but we have three who can do that."

"Can we have your Second, those three and three others. Your Second would be in charge of your people."

"Wait a moment and I'll summon her."

When the Second in command arrived the COS introduced everyone to Kristin Jungers and explained the mission. Jungers was a tall fit blond haired woman who appeared to exercise daily. She addressed Laura, "What and where do you want us?"

"The target group numbers are unknown, but is probably from three to ten people. They plan on burning the principle Catholic Church in Cologne early tomorrow morning. Hopefully, I can get better numbers before then. We will teleport our group there and wait inside for them to arrive. We plan on freezing them all in place and then turning them over to the European Union. Any questions?"

"Yes, why use us? I'm sure you two could handle this without our help."

"PR. These kooks are burning churches. We need to put ourselves out there as His instrument of punishment when someone defaces God's work. We need you there to show it's not just the Priestess's agents who work for God. When the vid networks show up it's going to be you and the EU Agents who get the accolades."

Laura turned to Sheila. "One of us will teleport you two back to the church to make arrangements for our arrival after mid-night mass. If you want to talk to us just think my name with concentration."

After James left with the two agents, Laura asked Kristin to assemble her six staff members so that she could access their abilities. James soon returned and with Laura they talked to the COS about any problems he had recently encountered while they waited for Kristin to return.

Kristin stuck her head into the room and asked them to follow her to a conference room. The six stood at attention as they entered the room. The four men and two women tried their best not to look at them while Kristin looked proudly at her people. "The women have the strongest powers including the ability to freeze. The man on the end also has this power along with strong telepathic abilities. The other men have slightly less telepathic powers."

Laura looked at Kristin with a raised eyebrow. "You have the strongest powers of the group."

At Kristin's nod they walked down the group until Laura stopped before one of the men and fingered a frayed cuff of his tunic. "Change this before we leave. I want you all to look sharp for the vid's. When we get to the church we will stay out of sight until the intruders arrive with their equipment. Don't move until you receive a mental signal, we want to make sure they are all inside before we freeze them. Any questions?"

One of the women asked, "Are you going to teleport us there?"

"Yes, it's no big deal, but you will have bragging rights for years to come. Nothing else? No, then Kristin has you until we are ready to leave."

Laura and James found a quiet place to surf minds until they found the conspirators again. Fifteen minutes later they both found separate sources thinking about the church burning. After the arsonists finished these thoughts Laura came out of her trance. Laura started to speak to her mate when she realized he was still connected, so she joined his thoughts.

Before she could eavesdrop her mate disconnected and smiled at her. "I got more information!"

Laura kissed James and hugged him tightly. "Me too, you go first."

"Well, according to my source he is to meet three others and then at two a.m. enter the church bringing several incendiary devices."

"My source was going to pick up four people in a stolen truck at one-thirty a.m. and deliver them to the church at two, then circle the block until they come out. We need to have someone freeze the truck and driver after it leaves the church. I'll talk to Kristin about tasking one of her girls for that, so let's go find her."

Using their powers they followed her mind glow until they found her with her charges. Getting her attention, Laura motioned for Kristin to join them in the hallway. They then moved beyond earshot before telling her what they had learned and asked, "How do you want to handle the truck driver?"

She raised an eyebrow at Laura. "I would wait until he made a circuit, but he might get away if they had a prearranged signal. So, I had better place one of my girls out of sight at the end of the block to freeze the vehicle and man in place."

"Good plan. I've already contacted the Union Agents and they suggested we arrive at one-fifteen. We will meet you and your team here at that time to teleport everyone to the church. We have about eight hours, so I suggest we all have a meal and rest before we leave."

Kristin smiled at them. "How long has it been since you've eaten?"

James shrugged his shoulders. "If you don't count a snack in Cologne this morning, about eight hours. I hope you have a place to eat here."

"Follow me and we'll all get something to eat. Do you like German food?"

After eating Kristin found quarters for them so they could rest and even provided a wake-up. Refreshed they joined the others and at the appointed time they teleported to the Cologne church. The Union agents met them and directed them to an out-of-sight place where they could observe anyone entering the church.

Twenty minutes later Kristin sent her designated staff member outside to get into position to handle the truck driver. The next fifteen minutes passed so slowly that everyone was checking the time. The front door opened and a man looked around checking if anyone was present before motioning that the way was clear. Three other people followed the leader inside, all carrying incendiary devices. Laura gave a mental command to freeze everyone in the group, and then checked with the team member outside.

"Kristin, your security person outside reports her mission was successful. I told her to come inside and join us."

The Union agents had already summoned the local police who arrived five minutes later. Laura and James let the others take the lead in explaining what happened and were just one of the team when the broadcast vid reporters arrived covering the capture of the people responsible for burning churches across Europe.

After the reporters had left and the police were satisfied that the European Union would handle the prosecution of the arsonists, everyone said their goodbyes to the Union Agents. The Priestess's Agents then teleported the security staff back to the Berlin Temple.

After Kristin assembled her staff, she had them come to attention then turned to address Laura and James. "It's been a pleasure to meet you two. You have lived up to your reputations and I hope to work with your teams in the future."

Laura smiled at her praise. "Thank you. Your team has brought honor to the Berlin Temple and I am sure that the High Priestess will personally acknowledge your contribution. We hope to see you again. Remember, God is watching over all of us."

Laura and her mate then teleported back to their apartment for a needed rest.

CHAPTER TWENTY-TWO

One year later both Laura and Lucy were large in their third trimester of pregnancy. Neither expectant mother had been on an assignment for over two months and were getting cabin fever. Their mates were kept busy taking care of them, while Aaron and Alice handled the assignments.

Between assignments, they were visiting their children who were together in Laura's apartment. The male halves of the pregnant couples appeared to be dazed by the whole experience and were getting in each other's way. Alice eventually told all the males to take a break and leave for a couple of hours.

Once the men left, all the women breathed a sigh of relief. Laura grimaced as she shifted positions in her chair. "Thanks mom, they were starting to get on my nerves. Would you get us all some hot tea to help us relax?"

Soon they were all sitting with a cup of tea in their hands and Lucy asked, "Alice, how in the world did you manage twins?"

"Aaron was a big help both before and after they were born. The real problem began when they came into their powers."

Both expectant mothers looked at Alice with wide eyes until Laura said, "And?"

Alice stuck out her tongue at Laura. "You were the worst! You were the leader thinking up things to bedevil me. I hope you get it back in spades for what you put me through."

"Aw mommy I'm sorry."

Then she had a thought. *I'm having a daughter. Oh my! Mom's right, the women are much more aggressive in our family.*

Seeing the expression on her daughter-in-law's face Alice shook her head. "Lucy, you may not have the same problems as Laura, but I wouldn't count on it. My advice, when they first start coming into their powers tell her what the rules are and come down hard on her if she willfully breaks them. Keep after her on the rules and explain why they must be followed."

Laura grimaced. "I still remember you upending the play pen over David and me, like a little jail. But then I finally got your point."

Lucy looked at the mother/daughter exchange in shock. "You're putting me on! That actually happened? How old were you?"

"About three, almost four. How old were you when you started getting your powers?"

"Much older, about ten. You talk like your powers were much stronger than mine. I couldn't throw things with my mind until I was twelve. Oh my, this can be bad. I'll have to ask David what you two did at that age."

"Don't be such a ninny! I had to deal with twins and I managed. If you get too frustrated just place a force field around the little monster and let her realize whose boss. I used the idea of a favorite treat reward if she behaves. For her it worked."

"Mom, I remember that. Even then I could tell how frustrated you were and I wanted the loving mom back, so I went along with your ploy."

"Oh honey! Maybe if I had pictured in your mind what could happen to you or David if your physic play went wrong. Do you think that would have worked?"

"Maybe, but a static shock would have worked quicker," Laura murmured as she rubbed her stomach.

Alice shook her head at her daughter. "You are so much smarter than me in some things, but right now what questions do you two have for me?"

* * *

Three years later Aaron and Alice were visiting Laura who had Lucy over for a play date for their children. Laura's daughter, Cynthia, was playing with Lucy's daughter, Kaitlin, while their mates were off together on assignment. The two girls looked like identical twins rather than cousins; partly because they were born a day apart and historically all Pearson women look alike.

Alice was happy to see that the two girls were concentrating on playing a simple pong style game of mentally bouncing a small ball back and forth. Cynthia looked at Alice and waved, mentally saying, *Hi Granma,* followed by Kaitlin's *Hi Aunt Alice*. They stopped the game and came over to get a kiss and hug from her.

"I don't remember you or David at their age being this mentally advanced. Do they carry on mental conversations with each other and other telepaths?"

"Yes, but I'm trying to get them to speak vocally. It's harder to get their vocal voice to work for them, so they generally use their mental voice."

"I understand that, but it's their reasoning ability that seems advanced for their age."

"Oh. You mean their greeting. I guess I'm a little too close to them. Now that I think about it they do communicate with us like a little adult, a thinking reasoning adult. Lucy, what do you think?"

Lucy was looking at them with wide startled eyes. "Oh my gosh! Our kids may be geniuses. Is there a way to test them at their age?"

Aaron interrupted, "You may be over reacting. Why not run your own tests documenting what your results are for a few months, then depending upon your results you can make a better decision."

* * *

Six months later the test results were back for Cynthia and Kaitlin. They both had almost identical powers as their parents, although weaker because of their age. Their IQ's were so high for their age they couldn't be determined.

"I'm glad that their healing powers haven't developed yet. Natalie will have to screen any future tests if she wants to keep this power a secret," Aaron pointed at the page as he handed the results to Alice.

"Honey, it seems each Pearson generation receives something new. I wonder what else our grandchildren are going to surprise us with?"

"Yes, I don't want to be in our kids' shoes raising those two; however, so far they have been two little angels."

* * *

Twelve years later Cynthia and Kaitlin were attending a special class for gifted students. The other two members, Ryan Stewart and Nathan Lewis, while considered to have genius IQ's in the high 150's were dwarfed compared to the girls IQ's of 178.

Ryan wadded up a piece of paper and waited until the instructor turned her back on the students, then quickly threw the wad at Cindy's head. The projectile did a u-turn six meters after leaving his hand and hit his head causing him to exclaim, "Ooh!"

Without turning the instructor said, "Mr. Stewart pick up that missile and place it in the waste bin. You and Miss Pearson will stay after class."

The two guilty parties said in unison, "Yes Ms. Parker."

Later, after class the two students stood before the instructor's desk. "Mr. Stewart were you so bored with the lesson that you felt the need to disrupt the class?"

Ryan's face turned red with embarrassment, then shrugging his shoulders said, "I was just getting back at her for what she did to me earlier."

"Miss Pearson, tell me what he's talking about."

"He pulled my hair, so I gave him a mental kick in the pants."

"Mr. Stewart based upon what I've observed you would be advised to cease your attacks against Miss Pearson. You are ill prepared for her counter attacks. Why not shake hands and stop this child's play before you get hurt."

Ryan looked at Cynthia and said, "Okay, I'm done. Friends?" He held out his hand.

Cynthia took his firm hand and they shook hands while looking into his eyes. *Ryan, we make better friends than enemies. Let this stop here and let's help each other in the future.*

Ryan nodded his head and gave her a slow smile as they released hands. Ms. Parker smiled at the two saying, "That's better. Now get out of here, I've got work to do."

The two teenagers walked to the temple's front entrance where they stopped. Ryan hesitated for a moment. "Cindy, would you like to come to my birthday party tomorrow at six p.m.? No presents, just other students interested in what you're and Kaitlin's parents do. Kaitlin has already agreed to come."

Cynthia looked into Ryan's eyes while gingerly mentally probing for any other reason for wanting her to attend the party. "Sure, where is your apartment located?"

"It's in building 12A, next to yours, apartment 10267. Wear something other than your Blues."

She raised her eyebrow at that comment. "What! Don't tell me you are one of those people who chafe at conformity."

His face flamed in embarrassment. "No, I just wanted to see you in something else. Well, I better call a robo cab. See you later."

They both stepped outside where he had a short wait for his ride. After he departed she teleported to her apartment. Both her parents were on assignment so she looked for a note from them. Finding none she checked the cooler for a snack and sat watching a vid until they returned.

She and Kaitlin had consulted on what they should wear and met in front of Ryan's apartment building. When Kaitlin arrived Cynthia was happy to see she was wearing what they had agreed upon. Kaitlin placed her hand over her mouth and snickered. "Oh Cindy you are sooo bad!"

When they approached the apartment door they both had to concentrate to keep from laughing. Mora Stuart answered the door and her eyes widened in surprise, then recognizing who they were quirked her mouth in a smile waving them inside. "Ryan! You have guests."

Ryan moved quickly into the room and stopped dead in his tracks in surprise where the two girls had struck a poise. "Wow! What era are you dressed for?"

Cynthia, still poising said, "Early twentieth century. It's supposed to be flapper dresses, what do you think?"

"Well, you don't have to worry about anyone beating this

getup. Who helped you with this?"

Kaitlin laughed. "This is all Cindy. She found a picture and had a replicator make one for each of us. I like it. Watch when I shimmy like this."

"Wow! It looks like your whole body is moving. Come on let's show the others."

The girls in the party mobbed the "twins", as they were nicknamed, to find where they could get their own. Cynthia and Kaitlin put on a little show dancing to the music of the era. Later, while eating birthday cake they answered questions from the group about past assignments of their family, especially any that they had participated in.

They told the others that the assignment to Mars to save the colony was their favorite. Cynthia related how her mother, Laura Pearson, had told her about her experiences there. How the silence was so surreal and the twin moons rising above her head bathed her surroundings in a golden glow. Then this was all shattered when the meteor approached roaring like a banshee as it passed overhead when their team diverted its path.

Kaitlin watched the faces of their little group at the retelling of a story they grew up with. Their faces reflected rapt concentration as Cynthia's words painted a visual picture in their minds, almost as if they were present. When the story ended they sighed in disappointment, looking with envy at them as the chosen ones who were born into this exciting life.

Later that evening after the girls left Ryan's apartment they stood outside the building and talked. Kaitlin looked up at the night sky and grimaced. "There is so much light pollution that you can hardly see any stars. Mom's memory of Mars' night sky is completely different. The stars were bright and sharp. The Milky Way she saw was something I've never seen here except in vid's. I wonder what it would be like to explore the Stars?"

"You've got the wanderlust. I'm going to ask Mom to task us with more work. I'm getting bored too."

They looked at each other and smiled, then teleported to Cynthia's apartment. Laura looked up at their arrival and smiled. "Did you have a good time? I bet those dresses were a hit."

"Mom, we're really bored. We need to be part of your team. Work us in because I know we are ready."

Laura looked at the girls' faces and determined stance for a moment, then smiled. "Okay, I'll bring your request before the others. Your grandparents are the ones you will have to convince."

The next day the entire team met to decide the girls' request. Aaron and Alice were now over sixty years old, but looked like they were in their early forties. In addition to good genes they had maintained an exercise program that kept them fit. Alice motioned for the girls to step forward. "So, you think you're ready to join us. What's the hurry? You're still in school."

Cynthia smiled at her grandmother. "School isn't enough anymore. We're really bored and we think we can contribute if you give us a chance."

Alice looked at their mothers and asked, "I know they're smart, but can they think through a problem if something changes the plan?"

Laura and Lucy looked at their daughters and smiled. "I think they need this test and we both think they are ready," Laura said with conviction.

Alice looked at the others. "All right! By a show of hands, do you all agree?"

Every team member raised his or her hand. "Very well girls. We will select an assignment for you and monitor how you perform. Any questions?"

The girls ran to Alice and hugged her tightly. Cynthia leaned back and looked into Alice's eyes. "I know we won't disappoint you."

CHAPTER TWENTY-THREE

Three days later Cynthia and Kaitlin were standing on a street in Atlanta, Georgia with their monitor, Grandmother Alice Pearson. She looked at the two girls with a small smile on her face.

"Okay, what's your plan?"

Cynthia mentally asked her cousin for permission to speak for them and at her nod said, "Well, our task is to find the people who are thinking about defacing the entrance to the Atlanta Temple. We plan on separating so we can get a fix on their location. When we locate the suspects, then we will strive to show them the error of their intentions."

"Very well, I'll go to the Temple and follow your thoughts until you are ready to confront them."

Fifteen minutes later the girls were standing in front of an older thirty-story apartment complex. Kaitlin looked up at the center building and smiled. "Looks like they are on the fifth floor and I read three minds. Is Grandmother on the way?"

Alice materialized just then and asked, "Tell me what you know and your plans to confront the people?"

Kaitlin told her their plans and how they wanted to confront them in their apartment.

"You say these three appear to be juveniles and there are no mature thoughts in the room. When you confront them how do you plan to change their minds?"

"With our powers of course," said Cynthia.

"Very well let's proceed and I'll observe."

Cynthia knocked on the apartment door where the thoughts originated. They could hear loud music originating from inside the room. Impatiently she pushed the buzzer and pounded on the door until it opened. A young male about their age stood before them.

He had a scowl on his face that quickly turned to a lecherous grin when he saw two apparently beautiful twin girls. "What can I do for you ladies? Step right in and can I get you something to drink?"

When Alice followed them inside and shut the door, he quickly became suspicious. "Buster, Tadpole look what we have here!"

Buster crowded closer asking, "What do they want Red?"

Cynthia smiled at them and gave them a small mental push backwards. "You boys have been having naughty thoughts about defacing the Healing Guild Temple."

Red's face flushed in anger as he shouted, "So what! You going to call your God down on us? I bet we can give you some fun if you ditch the older broad."

Cynthia froze in place the other two boys who were standing behind Red, who had no idea he was now alone facing the three females. She and Kaitlin levitated Red about three feet above the floor and started spinning him slowly, then faster as his face reflected his discomfort. This was quickly replaced by fear as the spin became faster and he started to loudly scream to the other boys for help.

The girls stopped the spin with Red's body upside down. Kaitlin's voice was edged with her apparent anger when she demanded, "What was your comment about my God? How much persuasion do you need to change your mind?"

"Ooh! I'm going to be sick. Go, go away. Please leave me alone. We weren't really going to do anything to the Temple. Buster and Tadpole would crap in their pants if anybody came after them. It was just talk to make us seem tough."

Cynthia released the boys who all scrambled away from them until they reached the far wall. "Think of us as God's right hand. If you even think about doing anything against a Healing Guild or

House of Worship you will receive another visit from us and we won't be nice. **Do you understand**?"

They all huddled together and trembled, then nodded their heads in agreement.

Alice and the girl's teleported back to the front of the building. Alice looked at the girls and said, "Wow! You made believers out of those boys. I give you both high marks for this assignment. Your next one will have more personal risk, but not too much as you haven't got your armor yet. You won't receive that until you get your growth."

The next day at school the other students wanted to know why they missed the previous class, so they made up a story about doing an evaluation for their future entry into their families' teams. Not a complete lie, but one that wouldn't solicit as much envy from the other students.

The girls, while emotionally close as if they were sisters, didn't want to be known as twins. So, they took pains not to dress the same after leaving the Temple - everyone wore Blues while in the Temple. Because of their beauty and heritage others constantly sought them out, but while this attraction stoked their egos they realized that this was due in large part to their inner aura. Their parents and grandparents all had to adjust their behavior because of this factor.

That evening the girls and their parents were summoned to Aaron and Alice's apartment. Upon arrival, Alice gave the girls' parents a mental replay of their assignment. When finished, Laura went over to Cynthia and Kaitlin and hugged them tightly followed closely by the other parents.

Alice cleared her throat getting their attention. "I think we can all agree that the children have demonstrated they are ready for some limited assignments. Even while angry they channeled their efforts toward achieving their goal of stopping further plots against the Temple. I think everyone agrees that goal was achieved."

Laura asked, "We can't send them out without supervision since they don't have armor, so what's the solution?"

Cynthia shrugged her shoulders before blurting, "We have been practicing placing a force field around us, but it's cumbersome. When we walk inside with the field it knocks things over."

Laura frowned in thought. "Have you tried to wear the field like a coat?"

Kaitlin rolled her eyes in frustration over this obvious solution before using her hands as a guide shaping the field around her body. "Hey! I think I did it. Cindy give me a mental punch."

There was a blur of movement on Kaitlin's shoulder as Cynthia's punch landed. "Wow, I knew something hit me, but it didn't hurt. I think this might work."

Alice shook her head. "Why didn't any of us think of this before?"

"Honey, we didn't need it until now," Aaron said as he shrugged his shoulders.

"Okay, at our next assignment the girls will watch and contribute if the opportunity arises. Everyone agree?"

Everyone on the team replied, "Yes!"

Two days later Laura and James Blake were on assignment in Philadelphia with the two girls. The Stinky File indicated a problem involving a possible bombing of a historic public building. The girls each paired with an adult and separated hoping to get a fix on the suspects.

The girls were the first to catch thoughts about a bombing and they were soon all standing outside an apartment complex ten kilometers from center city. Cynthia said, "The tall tower on the left is where the thoughts originate. Kats, what do you think, twenty-sixth floor?"

"Yeah. I count six minds in apartment 2648 and there seems to be some urgency in their thoughts."

Laura nodded her head in agreement. "Let's get up there before anyone leaves."

Five minutes later they were standing outside the door of their suspects reading their surface thoughts. Laura mentally told the girls to stay outside unless needed. She then mentally unlocked the door and they entered the room and immediately froze everyone in place.

They did a head count and found only five people. Laura mentally informed the girls they were missing one and to keep alert. She then discovered another mind nearby and turned in that direction when a woman spoke from the hallway. "I found it in the back closet…"

She stopped when she saw the two agents, but before she could take any action Laura froze her in place. "Girls come inside and shut the door!"

Kaitlin pointed at the woman in the hallway. "What's she holding? It looks like a remote controller."

Laura walked over and took the object from the woman's hand. "I think you're right. Search the apartment for explosives."

Later, after the search turned up nothing else they decided to search the suspects' minds for information. Laura asked Cynthia, "Who's better at this, you or Kaitlin?"

"About the same. Why not give us each a subject and see what we come up with?"

Cynthia was given the woman in the hallway and Kaitlin one of the older men. Ten minutes later Cynthia said, "I'm ready."

Laura smiled at her daughter. "Let's wait until Kaitlin finishes. I think she's about done."

Soon after Kaitlin nodded her head. "Okay, go ahead Cindy."

"Well, my subject's name is Mary Shepherd whose mate is Peter Welsh. I think he's the guy with a mustache. The explosives are stored at Thrifty Storage not far from here. The bomb maker is Peter Welsh who trained under Alex Kendrick, now locked up in Orbital One. My subject thinks they can extort credits and gain the release of Kendrick by threatening to blow up the Liberty Bell and the Freedom Hall complex. Your turn Kats."

"My guy is named Mark Parsons whose girlfriend is the redhead over there and goes by the name Gloria Hale. She's there inside person who works at the complex. He appears to be a little dimwitted and fancies himself as attractive to women. The other two are Janice Kendrick, the boss, and Willie Smith. She's the sister of Kendrick and is the force behind this attempt to free him. Smith is her boyfriend."

Laura smiled at the girls. "Well done, both of you. What do you recommend we do next?"

Cynthia and Kaitlin mentally conferred for a few minutes then turned toward her. Kaitlin held Cynthia's hand saying, "We think there is enough evidence for a conviction of a charge of extortion and attempted jailbreak based on the stored explosives, remote device, and our testimony of our mind probes. The possession of explosives is also a violation of law."

Cynthia asked tentatively, "We can testify at our age, can't we?"

"I think so. If not, we were also part of the mind probe and would be eligible to testify. If we all agree let's com the police."

Later, after statements had been taken and the suspects removed by the police they all teleported to Aaron and Alice's apartment. Alice arranged for pizza delivery while Aaron asked for comments on the girls' performance.

David Pearson gave a crooked smile, "I was surprised at how strong their ability was to find and read the suspects' minds. I couldn't discern how many minds were in the apartment. Laura how about you?"

"Yes, you're right. They are stronger telepaths than us. I could tell there were multiple people in the apartment, but not their exact number. Just how much detail did you two discern?"

Cynthia and Kaitlin looked at the others in surprise before Cynthia said, "We could tell there were three women and three men and their minds were in turmoil, like an argument or something was lost or missing. Later, when Shepherd brought the missing remote device into the room it was clear what was troubling them."

Alice asked, "How long have you two been this powerful?"

Kaitlin looked questionably at her cousin before responding. "We got this strength shortly after we were twelve, about three years ago. We've had to learn how to dampen input from outside our minds, especially telepathy. We can read thoughts of anyone we've had prior contact with from a great distance, maybe unlimited. It's possible we are stronger than any of you."

Their parents looked at the girls at first in shock, then with compassion as they remembered their own struggles living with their powers. Laura went to her daughter and hugged her tightly. "Oh honey you should have told us about your problems with your powers. We could have offered advice."

"Kaitlin and I helped each other, but we had someone else give us advice that really worked."

"Yeah," said Kaitlin. "She said her name was Barbara and was a close friend of our grandparents. She was dressed oddly though and afterwards she appeared to teleport elsewhere. Do you know who that was?"

Alice gave the grandchildren a slow smile. "We all know who the Angel Barbara is. Don't you remember the stories we told you as you were growing up?"

The girls looked at her in surprise. Cynthia blurted, "We thought you were telling us fairy tales. Really! That was Barbara?"

"Did Barbara say anything else that might be of interest to us?"

Kaitlin's eyes sparkled as she excitedly said, "Maybe. Now that we know she was Barbara this might be important. She said God has plans for Cynthia and me when we gain more experience. That's really vague and at the time we disregarded it."

Alice shook her head. "Historically Barbara's statements to us mere mortals are like that. Her recipients learned to ask questions in order to get clarity from her statements. When you see her next keep that in mind. In the meantime it appears that the girls are receiving the experience mentioned by Barbara, so I expect to hear from her soon."

Everyone was nodding their heads when Barbara appeared in front of them. "Well, I guess this is as good a time as I could expect. Kaitlin, Cynthia you both have exceeded my expectations and I'm proud of you as any Aunt would be. Aaron, Alice you have raised children any parent would envy and yours and their performance is almost beyond belief. Beginning with these girls there will be an emergence of a new breed of humans; intelligent, God fearing, and having empathy towards others. Now is the time for questions!"

Alice quickly asked, "I suspected that with each generation having greater powers that God was preparing us for some task, but this I was not expecting. What are your plans for the girls' future activities?"

"God expects you to continue as before, but wants you to establish satellite offices to eventually cover every continent on Earth. This probably can be accomplished in the next ten generations."

Cynthia asked, "That means many or all future mates will be from other continents. How will this be arranged?"

"By me of course. I've arranged for all of your mates. Has anyone been dissatisfied by my choices?"

All of the adults said a loud "no" that brought smiles from the two girls. Kaitlin asked, "Are we going to the stars?"

"When I was a girl I thought of Mars as one of the stars, but I'm sure you are referring to a destination outside this solar system. Maybe not in your lifetime, but soon man will leave this system to explore and expand its influence."

Barbara smiled at them. "I wish I was in your shoes as you experience the challenges in your future, but watching you is almost as fulfilling. Angel Pearson would have been proud of all of you."

Barbara nodded her head at them before disappearing.

ABOUT THE AUTHOR

Hugh A. Flowers retired after almost thirty years with the Federal Deposit Insurance Corporation as a bank examiner. He now spends his time reading and writing novels and short stories and traveling the world.

OTHER PUBLICATIONS BY FLOWERS

The SALVATION SERIES is a feel good story about people who are born into a destiny of God's making. They are guided throughout their lives by angels giving them instructions that sometimes are unclear as to their purpose, but reveal themselves as time progresses. Salvation is the first book in the trilogy; Angel's Triumph is the second: Third is In Perpetuity.

Reclamation, Oklahoma Tomboy, and Project Inception are also books written by Hugh.

www.ingramcontent.com/pod-product-compliance
Lightning Source LLC
Chambersburg PA
CBHW051241170626
46809CB00004B/1429